Truth Lies with Madness

E. S. Springer

I0548721

Truth Lies with Madness
Copyright © 2024 Erik Springer

Deepest thank you to those special folks who read this book as a draft, provided constructive feedback, and even contributed some great ideas to make this story the way it was meant to be.

What Sparks in the Dark

As it always did, the alarm went off. My time had ended. Just a few more minutes was all I needed, but the ringing in my ears ripped me away from my nap. I leaned over the bedside table, clumsily swiping off the crumpled bag of chips; simultaneously nicking a glass of water that shot over the side and down onto the mustard-colored carpet. I finally clicked the alarm button off, and surveyed the damage I had done. The water stain, which was only a few speckles, would evaporate eventually, so I had little motivation to sop it up. Somehow, within my groggy state, I made my way to the sink in the bathroom.

It wasn't much of a bathroom. Just barely enough room for a shitty shower and a toilet that was so cramped, when I used it, my knees became lodged into the cupboard underneath the leaky sink. I rubbed the mirror, hoping to wipe off some of the grime I had let flourish. The mirror's dirt was tenacious, even with elbow grease. My efforts were to no avail, as no amount of cleaning would repair the webbing of cracks that writhed like a parasitic worm tunneling across the reflective metal. Some pieces of the mirror were missing, but through the cracks and smudges, I was able to tame my bed hair and hopelessly rub at the dark circles under my eyes. After flicking off another cockroach from my toothbrush with loathing, I imagined blasting it with my loaded handgun hidden underneath my bed... a little something I borrowed from my mother's house once I realized the neighborhood I lived in wasn't as safe as I would have liked.

I found an unopened granola bar on my bureau that would at least curb my hunger. I checked the clock one more time, grabbed a wad of cash left from my last paycheck, and headed for the door, which I opened and immediately closed, starting my ritual. Again, I opened the door, and again, I shut it. It was two more times before I felt satisfied and well enough to pass through the threshold.

A quick nap after a long ten-hour day working in St. Elizabeth's psych hospital was not enough to revitalize me for the remainder of the evening. A new person had been admitted to the hospital this morning, forced in by his mother, screaming and writhing as he entered. One of his arms had lashed out and bruised one of the staff, and I had no choice but to strap him into the gurney. His mother said he had gone crazy, and she feared for her life as well as his. Upon further questioning, she revealed to me that he had a history of schizophrenia, paranoia, hallucinations... the list continued. Whenever a new patient was admitted to the hospital, it was always a longer day than usual.

My father, the reason I do what I do for a living, also occasionally had tendencies toward hysteria, or at least that is what my mother told me whenever there was a chance. I remember he and I used to play checkers, chess, and games that required a more intellectual approach. He enjoyed them, so I enjoyed them. Nevertheless, he'd play my games too, like hide and seek. My sister Jane wouldn't play with me; she was always too busy doing whatever older girls did. With no other sibling to play with, I'd often find Freddy who was always in the mood to play, day or night. My father welcomed my friend, which made our ordinarily one-on-one hide and seek adventures more thrilling. My mother hated Freddy, but she didn't often like much of anything or anyone but Jane.

Just before I turned twelve, my father would frequently leave the house outside of typical working hours, gone for stretches at a time, until one day when he never came back at all. I remember that day so vividly: the olive-green dish towel that adorned the oven handle in the kitchen and the smell of chicken pot pie. Perhaps I don't remember that day so vividly; just the olive-green towel and the thick smell of chicken while we waited for him to come home and use the towel after washing his hands and before sitting down to eat our chicken meal. He never did. Freddy's visits reduced dramatically once my father left; I had no time to play anymore.

My mother's persistent accusations against my father's mental stability, especially after the night he never came home, were meant to dissolve my brain like a weak acid; corrosive but over years. Instead of absorbing her disdain, I fought against it by helping others like my father in any way I could. Now a decade later, I'm making a living, though not much of one, helping those who need all the love and support they can get while staying in a psychiatric hospital.

Sometimes, I feel like I need someone to help me though. I'm not a morning person. I hate them. Mornings are just like this afternoon's nap... the sheets lay heavy on me. Massive feather clouds that sink and keep me under and breathless. It feels good to be engulfed. Air above and springs below; a deceitful invitation to go up, not down. My bed's gravitational pull could suck me away. It wouldn't be too bad after all. Sometimes I can leave. Sometimes I can't. What is for sure, though, is the outside, or really reality can be so hollow. It's the shadow of my world and I'm not sure if I want to see it, ignore it, or hide.

After opening and closing the door a satisfactory number of times, I turned to lock my door from the decrepit hallway, which seems like it had never been updated or washed since it was built. As I did this,

I noticed a piece of paper taped over my door's peephole. I peeled it away, leaving behind adhesive residue, and read: *Eviction Notice: All rent must be paid by the end of the month. If occupant fails to fulfill all owed rent by this time, they will be escorted off the premises and legal action will follow.*

I scoffed, crumpling the paper and tossing it down the hallway. I had no time to deal with that bullshit. Let them take me away, any place would be better than this shithole. Since the building lacked an elevator, I descended the stairwell, skipping a few of the battered wooden steps that might not have carried my weight without breaking. Just the other day, another occupant of the building experienced an accident where they had fallen through the east stairwell. Poor bastard popped a hip out of its socket and broke the other leg on the way down. I didn't have time for that, or the bills that would surface after an emergency room visit.

The sun's limited rays had come and gone for the day while I was busy with my nap; the light had raced far ahead while the night trickled in behind it. It was drizzling, the spritz of rain practically indiscernible in the night and only visible within the globed auras of the blinking street lights. My eyes flickered as the drizzle tickled my eyelashes. For weeks the weather had not changed, with ever relentless rain and heavy fog in the morning and evenings. The time where the daylight reigned was decreasing each day as the season drew closer to winter.

My foot slipped against the harsh edge of a pothole, and a sharp pain splintered through my heel and into my ankle. I cursed, not at the pain wrecking my ankle bone, but at the shithole of a neighborhood. Every week, there was a new pothole, looming underneath and waiting to fell an unsuspecting prey. The pavement was cracked and stamped to mere gravel. Despite the lack of vehicular traffic, the creation of potholes and deprecation of the pavement steadily grew worse. Its deterioration seemed like my grimy mirror: hopeless to fix.

It wasn't just the roads. The neighborhood was full of crumbling, dilapidated housing. Miserable and gray; the only sign of life was the faint glowing of light behind the filthy curtains of a window or two. Fire escape staircases lay in shambles, littering the dull sidewalks, and the patches of grass surrounding small listless trees were brown and splotchy, lightly sprinkled with yesterday's shriveled leaves.

Out of habit, I stepped off the sidewalk and into the street without bothering to look both ways. But, like a moth, instinct guided my eyes to the traffic lights. The red light across the street seemed far and distant through the fog. Its red flare spread into lined rays, but then faded, becoming engulfed in the nightly fog.

"There it is! There! That's where you need to go!" I looked up to see the wilted, raggedy man with mud-soaked clothes crying out to me, just as he did every time I passed him sitting atop a large pile of abandoned rubber tires. He almost toppled off his rubber tower as he once again exclaimed, "Just there, listen to me, I can help you!" The man pointed down the sloping road that scaled through more battered buildings.

I ignored the haggard man as best I could, focusing instead on the drizzle splattering my face and on maintaining a foothold on the pavement. But like the alarm clock, the man's voice split my brain in half. After I hurried my steps and traveled another block, the haggard man's voice trailed away, to be replaced with a deep crunch sound as suddenly all the lamp lights went out.

The complete darkness startled me, caught me off guard, and my senses became discombobulated. Even though I stood still, my eyes searched around until they adjusted to the darkness, and clarity once again came back to me. I glared up at the dead street lights, scratching my arm, and thought about whether the electrical company even knew the lights had gone out, which only raised my ire.

I took a careful step down and off the curb, but paused as I heard the undisputed tapping of a woman's heel against the pavement behind me. Out of instinct, I crooked my neck and saw the silhouette of a dark figure, clothed in a wandering dress. It wasn't often I met someone else traveling among the worn streets, other than the haggard man that seemed to always be propped on his pile of tires.

The black billowing garments became more in focus as she rapidly approached. I couldn't help but stare. When she passed me, I could smell her perfume. Our eyes linked, and for the briefest of moments, she slowed her pace. Her eyes were on fire, her nose sharp, and her cheeks sullen. The darkness did nothing to hide her magnificence. Then, with a flutter of beautiful eyelashes, the moment was over and she swept away, quickening her pace.

A short static eruption, and the traffic light turned back on, gleaming its red orb. I realized I had stopped dead in the middle of the street. The light fixtures turned on in turn, illuminating a shadow behind her as she marched away. As reality set in, its gloom weighed heavily on my shoulders.

Mother of Mine

Once I reached the outskirts of the shithole, I was lucky to catch a short cab ride the rest of the way to my destination. The taxi stopped in front of my mother's rowhouse. I grabbed at my pockets and paid the taxi driver. Luckily, the miles gauge on the dashboard wasn't high. My paycheck was already disintegrating away. I held my breath, careful not to breathe in the noxious fumes from the taxi as it peeled away. I fumbled with my keys, unlocked the front door, and started my ritual. Opening and closing enough times to feel the avalanche of calm before stepping through the doorway.

"Boy? Is that you?" came my mother's shrill call from the living room. I responded with a grunt, sliding off my shoes and placing them by the umbrella stand. I made my way through the hallway, past the stairwell that led to the floors above. The same stairwell Fred and I would run down, my father's counting dwindling behind us as we searched for a place to hide.

Before I made it to the kitchen, I stopped at the display cabinet against the wall. I fiddled with my keys, and picked out a heavy black barrel key to unlock it. Inside were fragile ceramic pieces depicting young children in different poses and outfits. They stared, hollow eyed, with vacant smiles and dimples. One of the pieces, a little boy in a red rain jacket and boots, seemed just slightly out of its normal place, so I moved it a touch, just enough to put it back into its rightful position. Although I was not fond of the clay figurines, I preferred that they be situated properly. Certain things must have an order, and the wretched figurines were not spared.

Once I was satisfied with the figurines' arrangement, after moving a few other pieces back slightly away from the glass, I locked the display cabinet and made my way into the kitchen. I inspected the refrigerator and called out, "Have you eaten yet?"

"What kind of question is that?" barked my mother from the other room. "You know damn well I can hardly walk."

"You can when you really want to," I muttered, a little too loudly.

"What was that, Boy?"

I raced ahead, speaking loudly to avoid her question. "Looks like there really isn't much in the refrigerator, how about the leftovers from that steak dinner I made a few nights ago?"

I heard a "WRAH!" of disgust from my mother, and made my way to the living room where she sat in her plush armchair, a tennis ball walker an arm's length away. "There's eggs in there," she said.

"And how would you know that? I thought you could hardly walk?"

She crossed her arms with another "WRAH!" She waved her bony wrist and said, "Use the eggs, make them into an omelet, they've been in there for a few weeks now, it's about time they get used."

A voice in my head said I shouldn't use the eggs. I tried once more for the leftover option, saying that the steak was still good and it would spoil in a day or so and go to waste. She retorted with, "So will the eggs." I reluctantly gave in to her demands, but as I turned toward the kitchen she said, "Is there bacon?"

"What? I don't know, I can't remember," I said.

"If there is, you should put bacon in with the omelet. I need my protein, you know."

"Mom, there's protein in eggs." I felt my eyes begin to roll, but caught them, and instead pretended to look at the ceiling as if it were suddenly interesting.

"Don't get wise with me, crazy boy! Your father was the same way, but your sister... now she had it right. A smart girl, sweet girl, pretty girl..." Her eyes had glazed over, and a shadow of sadness crept over her face. But she snapped out of her trance when her eyes fell upon me, "What are you waiting for?"

I retreated back into the kitchen and began making her the omelet. Though I searched, there wasn't any more bacon left, so I cut tiny pieces of the leftover steak in my best attempt to simulate bacon. Ever since her brain tumor was removed a few years ago, her sense of taste had diminished considerably, but her eyesight was as keen as ever.

My cell phone rang. I quickly set the finished omelet in front of my mother, who thanked me with a curt "Where's the salt?" I ignored her, and instead dug into my pocket. I flipped the old battered phone open to see if I could catch a glimpse of the caller ID, but it was no use. The phone had been through many fumbles, which consequently inhibited much of the screen's display. I placed the receiver over my ear and answered the call, but there was no reply on the other end. "Hello?" I repeated, but still no response, so I shrugged, hung up, and went to fetch the salt, which was then poured liberally over my mother's omelet. As soon as I had placed the salt back in the kitchen, my phone rang again.

"Hello?" Again, no response, but as I pulled the receiver from my ear I heard the familiar voice. "Hey, baby, you coming to the club tonight?"

It was Valery, the other, much more loving, woman in my life.

My mind's eye reminded me of the eviction notice that had been taped to my apartment door. "Yeah, I'm coming. I need to make the extra money." I couldn't say any more, I didn't want Valery to worry.

And if my eavesdropping mother caught a whiff of a potential eviction, she would roast me with that knowledge like a marshmallow over a campfire; slowly until my insides melted. She would say, "Your sister never got evicted!" And likely she would make up the fact that my father was evicted three times, and I was on his hellish path... a phrase she had a certain predilection for.

Valery jerked my attention back to the conversation by saying, "Okay, great, I'll see you at The Rec Room then. Oh, and one more thing. Before you go to the club, can you stop by the store and pick out four eggs for me? Just drop them off at my apartment, you still have my spare key, right? I'm making brownies, but I'm fresh out of eggs, and the grocery store won't be open by the time I get off work. Thanks! Bye."

Nail of a Cowboy

"I gotta ask, you packing any heat?" I knew the man who stepped from the shadows into the blinding light of the street light, chewing nicotine gum. It was Patty, a good friend, a bit too rule oriented, but he always kept an eye on me. Two other larger men remained looming behind Patty, their massive arms crossed, but I paid little attention to them. I was no threat and they weren't a threat to me as long as I followed their rules.

"Really?" I shrugged at Patty as he began to check me for weapons.

"I know, I know, but I gotta do it," he whispered, gesturing lightly toward a camera in the ceiling corner. "I don't think you even own a gun, do you? You know you probably should. The people you hang about with here. I dunno, you never know what's out to get you. Anyway, gotta pat you down though." He gestured again to the camera. "Always being watched, just hold steady and put your arms up. Great, thanks."

"How late are you working tonight?" I asked.

"All night." Patty shrugged. "Every night until Wednesday, you free to catch up then?" I nodded, and he continued, "Cool. By the way, the word's 'poodle' tonight. There's a big guy in town, you know the kind. To get to that table just say you know William, they should let you in."

I nodded my understanding, and one of the bouncers opened the door for me. I entered the small shabby lobby adorned with fake plants and a top-loading water cooler illuminated by bleak fluorescent lighting. The club was hidden to most people so what was inside was special to those who had a pass. Wasn't easy for most to get in either; you had to prove your worth. Typically, you'd have to get a referral from someone who already knew of the place. Bleak fluorescent lights on the low, encased ceiling flickered enough to warrant an extra blink of an eye to adjust my sight. It still didn't help the flickering. An elderly man with a wide mustache sat behind a desk with mounds of stacked papers. He grumbled, licking his index finger and stamping a paper. His eyes were droopy and pink but they watched me closely underneath fluffy eyebrows. I said the passcode of the week in nonchalant disregard, "Poodle."

His fluffy caterpillars rose. "I see. Identification, please."

I showed him my driver's license and asked, "Where's Val tonight? Is she on the floor?"

Unsure how he could see through his caterpillar eyebrows I placed my license safely back in its proper place in my wallet. "Let me check." He clicked around on the nearby desktop before grunting, "I see here that she is scheduled to the bar this evening. You can cozy up at the bar, mind you don't get too handsy, or is there someone else you were hoping to see, maybe something more private? If you've got the money, that is."

I quickly shot down his advertisement, but said, "Actually, there's a special game tonight. William and I are buds, so he got me a seat." He eyed me, and sneered. "William who?"

I was quick on my feet, hiding how little I knew. "I can't tell you that." It wasn't a lie, but I held my breath. He glared at me, squinting me up and down, then cracked what I thought was a smile, instead it looked more like an opossum displaying its teeth, "He'll be setting up soon."

I wish I had asked Paddy for more details about this guy's poker game. I couldn't give myself away. I had to get to that table. That was the table where I could make enough money in just a few hours if I played my cards right.

With a sour growl of "Off you go then," he gestured his head to the steel door opposite the water tank.

The door buzzed, allowing me access, but after opening the door, I shut it before walking through. The buzz ceased. I gripped the handlebar and pulled, but it wouldn't budge, and I felt the nefarious tickle of sweat on my neck. I looked back at the old man who was hunched over his papers. Looking at me beneath those unkempt eyebrows, he pressed the buzz button again. Just as before I continued my ritual. And again, I looked back at the man. "Can you just keep pressing the button, please?" I asked, frustrated that my ritual was prolonged.

"Can't you just open the door and go through, *please*?" he mocked. "Good Lord, son, how long are you gonna be?"

"Not long," I said with a voice that should have shook less. When he jabbed underneath the desk again, I released my breath, relieved to be able to finish my routine.

The door shut behind me, and I inhaled the familiar stench. The air was moist, almost as humid as the fog outside, but with healthy additions of sweat, sex, and smoke. I walked along the once-red carpet, which was now muddled and brown, but the untrodden edges remained bright and unscathed. I went down the corridor, careful to avoid the splotches, stepping instead on the clean edges. The corridor led toward the rec room where the bar was serving drinks, poker tables were littered with chips and cards, and dozens of sofas and comfy chairs were scattered about the dark room. The tables looked normal tonight so far with the typical arrangement of folks I've seen before, mingled with a few new bland faces; nothing that displayed a first-class table, which meant I was early just as the front desk man indicated.

I made my way through the large rec room, where sweating drinks were temporarily forgotten on abandoned but lavishly adorned tables while people chatted to one another underneath the pumping music and glanced at the television that hung near the bar. It was a sophisticated façade, hiding its true visceral nature. I wandered through the labyrinth until I reached the bar.

Valery's back was toward me. She was busy making a concoction, and although I was anxious to delve deeper into the club and play a few hands at other tables to test the waters before the game with William, I took a bar stool. "I'll be right with you," she said without turning to me, focused on her task. I waited patiently and admired her from across the bar. Her hair was pulled back in a disordered bun, but her bangs remained down and over one eye. She was far too pretty to be with a guy like me. But she never seemed to mind. Sure, she looked great, but what kept me looking forward to seeing her was she always believed in me. She was the magnetic field to my compass, a support of which I had never unconditionally experienced previously. After she had divided up the drink into two martini glasses and handed them off to her customers, she turned to me, the red neon lights above the lounge reflecting in her eyes.

"Hey, baby." She leaned over the counter for a hug. "Want to try something new? Maybe your usual isn't working quite right for you?" For days, even weeks, I had a certain predilection for rum and cola. For some reason, it kept me in the zone, and I accredited the specific drink for all the winning games I had. But those nights were too far in the past. Perhaps it was time I tried a new drink; a new lucky drink. But really, I was just a sucker for her. "Am I going to be your guinea pig again?"

Valery clapped her hands when I gave a yielding nod, "Okay, so, I was thinking of making up something special." She rolled up her sleeves, revealing numerous tattoos, some concealing wounds from her past. "Turn around, let me see here…" I complied, and again waited patiently. My mind wandered, planning my attack at the poker table. I have to get a feel for the table, for the players, how they play but more so how they react to me. I can only control myself, not the cards or the people. Bluff early with a predicted loss, get an idea of what—

"There!" She placed a short glass in front of me, filled with swirling liquid, jerking me away from my thoughts. I gave the liquid in the glass an apprehensive inspection, but the red neon lights camouflaged its true nature. I took a sip. It tasted of soggy rats with a bite of cranberry. My eyes began to water and I turned away from the bar, hoping she wouldn't see my disgust. But I had failed. "That bad, huh? Here," she filled a glass full of water, "let that help you get the medicine down. I'll get you a rum and cola."

I pretended to not hastily chug down the water, which felt so smooth down my throat. The rum and cola felt right as it easily passed the corners of my tongue, sliding down until it warmed my chest.

"So," she began, "I can't really hang out much tonight, seeing as I'm going to be kind of busy all night, but how about you come over to my place tomorrow after work?"

Crestfallen, I said, "Actually, my mother's nurse called out sick, so I'll have to take care of her that night. . ." and I noticed she felt the same disappointment so I offered, "… but maybe I can swing by for a bit after work, then we can have dinner at my mother's?"

Her face contorted upon the invitation. "Ugh. You know she hates me. I don't think that'd be a good idea."

I preferred not to admit it, but my mother's disdain for my girlfriend was far from inconspicuous. Backhanded compliments, snide comments, and downright rudeness was the pinnacle of my mother's friendliness toward Valery.

I lied, "That was one time, and that was some time ago. Maybe if she'd just get to know you…" I began, but Valery cut in. "You mean, if she can look past what I look like?"

My eyes wandered to the black piercings in Valery's dimpled cheeks, and the luxurious art on her chest and arms. Even I couldn't rebuke Valery's statement, but I tried; I had to. "She wasn't always this harsh. Before the brain tumor she used to be much more lighthearted."

Valery gave a smile. "I just don't like it when she compares me to your sister. I get it though, she's been through a lot, after your father went away and your sister died, she must feel like she's to blame—"

I snorted, "I doubt she blames herself. You've heard her compare me to my sister and my dad. It's just what she does." I didn't want the conversation to continue any longer, so I broke it off with a curt, "Well, I should get to it." As I said it, I heard in my words a faint bite of my mother's harshness. In atonement, I smiled and kissed her goodbye over the counter, after an angry patron complained he had been waiting too long for her to take his drink order.

"So, I'll see you tomorrow after work?" she said with a faint smile as she poured a frothy beer from the tap.

Drink in hand, cash in my pocket; it was time to make some real money.

The night started terribly. After losing several

throws, the sweat began, but after a lucky shot and a quick but strong win, I was back on track. Nevertheless, I felt my luck was draining at the craps table, so I eyed the poker tables. A gregarious cowboy I had never seen before, evidently a talented player, or extremely lucky, clearly had domain over the table. His chips were piled high, greed gushed from his eyes. It leached into his laugh lines that never faltered, as if playing cards was just a game, and not something his life heavily relied on. It had to be William. The new hotshot in town.

I approached the table, and scowled up at the television above, annoyed that they would even put such a distracting thing above a poker table. But then, I realize perhaps this was William's doing: a trick, a distraction. This was someone who needed to lose.

I sat in an empty chair and addressed the dealer, "I'm in, next round."

They peered up at me, suspicion looming in their eyes. But the cowboy split a smile, welcoming me with fiery eyes. He saw a new challenge. I was up to bat and ready to swing a homerun. Instead of following the voice in my head, I decided to go with my gut. The first few hands gave me nothing. And while my pile of chips was slowly dwindling, the next deal gave me a good hand.

I shook my head. I needed to focus this round. I glanced again at my cards... not unexpectedly, they were still two queens. I eyed the table, looking for a twitch, but the players were adept. I couldn't read them; all I could hope for was that they couldn't read me either. I waited for the flop, which gave me nothing to add to my hand. Still, what was revealed could not beat my pair. Again, as if I had forgotten, I looked down at my cards, flipping the coated edges slightly to bring the red Q's to my view.

Th-thump. Th-thu-thump.

Quizzical, I focused my attention across the table toward the sound. The finger of the cowboy was quivering. At first, it seemed a nervous twitch, but as the betting continued, preceding the next card, its pace quickened. I looked around the table, but no one was reacting; not even a flick of an eye toward his finger. The cowboy's wide-eyed grin, irreversibly etched into his face, never quivered. SHOW A StuMP OF ThE FINGER OF ThE COWBOY.

Th-th-th-th-thump. It tapped even faster until it was inhumanly vibrating against the table, and still no one else reacted. They remained quiet, entirely absorbed in the game at hand. The vibrating escalated as the next card was revealed. I glanced at the pool of cards, but my eyes were magnetized, and reverted to the cowboy's vibrating finger. The speed at which the finger vibrated now obscured any of its detail.

Now, the river was revealed. *Th-th-th-th-TH-*

TH-TH. A measly three of clubs. A cold breeze prickled the table. *THMP-THMP-THMP-THMP.* The finger suddenly ceased with a final thud.

"*PULL IT!*"

The cowboy never flinched, instead maintaining a garish grin; flecks of red speckled his white hat and flung across the green felt, staining the cards. In the center of the table, among the piles of chips, was his fingernail. I stared in horror. The cowboy's grin emulated that of the figurines in the display case, and I tried not to scream. Did anyone care? The dealer calmly said to me, "Sir, it's your bet," and pointed to the chip pile, topped with the cowboy's fingernail. As he glanced at the pile, there was a ghastly mush and I saw the dealer's eyes redden, veins expanding until the whites were entirely bloodied then imploded, spurting more blood across the table and upon the fingernail atop the pile of chips.

Despite everything, all eyes were on me. I could feel them, their laser eyes piercing my face, and yet those laser eyes should be transfixed in horror at the blood-stained table. I felt like an alien. Did I really want to win a pot with an amputated finger at its crest? An appendage that no one seemed to mind was currently gushing blood, soaking into the poker chips. My hands trembling, I gave up my cards to the blinded dealer, folding the round.

"Keep dealing, dealer," the cowboy said, "the night's far from over. And, boy, do I feel great; like a winner!" He looked at me with a wild smile. "Since you're bailing so early, you owe me a drink next time."

Patient

I shoved a dollar bill into the machine, but it spat it back out. I groaned, squeezing it between my index and middle finger to flatten the tenacious creases. The machine ate it up this time, and I pressed the button titled "Cream and Sugar." However, what was dispensed into my cup seemed to lack both ingredients. I gave the coffee machine a dirty look and a solid kick with my toe.

I slept like a baby last night, despite what I had witnessed. I told Valery about the cowboy and the incident at the poker table, but she didn't think much of it. She told me I just needed more sleep and gave me a few pills that knocked me out cold. They worked alright, perhaps a bit too well, since now it was midday, and my feet felt like they were dragging a half a mile behind me. I needed a caffeine boost; admittedly unusual, for I rarely indulged in a cup of coffee. The taste was unsettling; nothing that dark, bitter, and hot should ever be consumed. Thus, the gratuitous amounts of cream and sugar I added whenever I indulged in a dreadful cup.

I didn't have an office, or a cubicle, so I sat myself on one of the benches in one of the hallways. We had a staff room, but there never seemed to be enough seats. The other staff were apologetic that there were no seats, but never offered me one. It was too loud anyway.

Those who couldn't fit in the staff room ate with the patients. Many of the patients required constant attention, which was covered by shifts of two or three. Today, I was free for the lunch hour, so I quietly sipped my coffee. Out of habit, I checked my pager, which was refreshingly empty.

While most of the staff were designated to certain patients, I made an effort to familiarize myself with many of the patients wandering the halls. Sometimes, all they needed was a listening ear or a kind chat, which occasionally erupted into gossip. This accusation I make primarily toward Isabel, a middle-aged woman with silver streaks in her long mane. Her stay at the hospital was likely permanent as she was an unstable paranoid schizophrenic from sector 2B. Every other day someone else in the hospital, whether that be another patient or a staff member, was plotting to kill her, poison her, or find all her secrets. On the other days, it was the government conniving all sorts of things to her. Quite naturally, they had tremendous intrigue in the likes of her, and often the staff members were secret agents watching her every move.

As if she knew I had been thinking of her, Isabel appeared down the hallway, her overly long black skirt skidding its faded edges against the tile. She walked by me without a word, focused elsewhere in her mind. But then she stopped suddenly, cranking her neck around to face me like an owl. I couldn't help but flinch at her fierce gaze. Her eyes bulged so scarily that I half expected them to pop out and dribble across the tiled floor... my mind's eye recalling the blood red eyes of the dealer being crushed. Her gaze was so intense that I averted my attention to sipping my coffee, hoping she would pass by.... I was too much of an optimist. She finally rotated her body to match her head, and began to slouch toward me.

"How are you today, Isabel?" I asked, trying to ease the tension.

She batted the air and shushed me. She crept closer, her arms poised like a raptor ready to strike. Her nostrils began to flare, and I realized she was sniffing as she came closer. I looked down at my coffee, saw the steam wafting away. "It's just coffee," I said, lifting the cup to show her. She tried to bat it out of the air, and I almost lost my grip. Coffee splashed on my shoes, and I felt it seep into my socks. "Isabel!" I exclaimed, but her intense sniffing stopped my exclamation dead.

She looked over my shoulder and gasped, holding a hand over her mouth and nose. With a shiver, I looked behind me, but all I saw was an empty hallway. "Isabel, do you want me to escort you back to your room?"

She calmed down almost instantly, her eyes receding back into her head. Normalcy somehow returned as if a switch flipped, and for a second, I could see a sign of her younger self. "Oh, darling, that would be wonderful. Would you mind? I've seen enough for one day."

As I brought her around the corridor, I asked, "Isabel, when is your husband's next visit?"

"Oh," she said with a faint whisper, "I think maybe in a few days. You know, he's been quite busy at the office this past month. Did you hear, though? Did you hear about what Harry did?"

I sighed, but fed her craving. "No, Isabel, what did Harrison do?"

"I heard that Harry, well," she squirmed uncomfortably, "he put his you know what in the rice pudding this morning. No one should eat the rice pudding tonight. He's trying to poison us. You know how he is, he's very dangerous and I'm sure he has it out for me."

"Harrison isn't even in your sector, you hardly see him. I'm sure he likes you well enough."

"Harry likes me?!" she gasped. "Oh gosh, that's even worse! He's trying to seduce me. It all makes sense now! He wants to drug me, then have his way with me tonight after I eat the rice pudding." She fluttered her eyelashes. "Oh, I guess it could be worse. You know he is a strong, handsome man…"

Thankfully, we arrived at sector 2B and, after

my ritual, I finally opened the door for her. She entered, but kept her foot on the threshold. "Rumor has it that he put it in everyone else's pudding too; not just mine. Check it will you?" I assured her I would check the kitchen immediately, and with a contented smile she withdrew her foot. I closed the door gently and turned, but the door ricocheted back against my heel. I staggered back to see Isabel had opened the door. Her eyes were bulging again and she said in a clear and resolute voice, "Young man, listen." I tried to back away, but she darted forward and grasped my shirt, wrenching me so close to her bulging eyes that I could smell her breath. "Beware of the bill. Keep your limbs about you. Listen, see, and learn, or ignore and yearn." Her eyes receded, as did her grip on me, and she disappeared behind the door of sector 2B.

A shroud of silence enveloped me, making me shiver. I had little time to catch my bearings before my pager buzzed. I was needed back in sector 4. It was Brian who needed attention. I wasn't surprised. Newer patients, beginning their psychotropic medications, frequently had difficulty acclimating to their new surroundings. Brian had come in on his own accord. He was a large fellow, but thankfully calm. When the staff asked why he was admitting himself into the hospital, he had simply responded by asking us to keep an eye on him, because something bad might happen. At first, we asked for more information, even directing him to the police if he truly thought he was in danger. But he insisted, refusing to leave the hospital, saying that this was the safest place for him to be. I wondered, did that something "bad" happen? Perhaps Isabel was right, I thought with a mirthful smile, maybe someone was poisoning people after all.

When I arrived, Brian was sitting on the floor, looking up at the staff surrounding him. They appeared apprehensive and timid to approach him more closely, as if they worried another step forward would trigger a hidden mine. "What happened?" I asked.

A staff member named Sarah said, "He just started screaming and shaking his arms. He kept screaming something was on him, he ran around like crazy. He even knocked over one of our interns." She pointed to one of the staff members nursing an elbow.

"Just give him a moment; give him some air." The staff didn't need me to say it twice. The circle around Brian widened. I squatted down beside Brian, who was breathing heavily, recovering from the episode.

"How are you feeling, Brian?" I asked.

He looked at me, his pupils dilated but shrinking back down. "It was on me. I couldn't get it off, but it's off now, circling…" I understood his panic. The anxiety and stress controlled his voice.

"Well, good, I guess. How do you feel now?"

"Much better, now that it's not hooked on me anymore, stalking." His shoulders fell as his body began to relax more.

"What is 'it'?"

His eyes unfocused, looking behind me, "I'm not sure what it is. But here..." He fumbled within his pockets and withdrew a pair of sunglasses. "You should have these. You need them."

"Oh thanks, Brian." I said with a pretend smile. "I'll keep them well and safe."

"Good," he said. "Because now It's watching you."

My spine tingled and my shoulders pricked.

"Well, Brian," I said, trying to shake off what he had said, "thank you again for the sunglasses, and I'm glad you are feeling—" Brian stiffened. His mouth opened partially, a sliver between his lips, and he started to moan a single note at almost a whisper. I leaned in, thinking he was trying to say something quietly, but his mouth opened more, and the note became louder and more powerful. I tried calming him down, but his eyes were unfocused, looking behind me. His mouth gaped open, and his voice increased in intensity and became ear splitting. I bolted across the room to a medical closet and swiped my key card, but the door wouldn't open, and coupled with Brian's ear-splitting drone, I began to panic.

Sarah came up behind me and said, "I can do it, you shouldn't be going in there anyway. Go back with Brian, try to calm him down. I'll get the sedative." She swiped her key card, and the door clicked open.

It wasn't long before Sarah returned, sticking a needle into Brian. Gradually his drone decreased steadily until his mouth shut and his head bobbed. "Let's get him back to his room," Sarah said, and together we picked him up and helped him stagger to his room.

Apartment 301

I clunked the third floor button with the side of my fist. As the doors closed, I was compelled to press the "close door" button four times. I easily pressed the button in quick succession enough times before the lethargic elevator doors finally closed, and I felt a fleeting weight in my head from the sudden motion of the elevator as it rose. I sighed, enjoying the calmness of the elevator ride and lamenting the broken one in my own apartment. The hallways in Valery's building were clean and orderly with occasional cushioned wooden benches waiting to be used. The walls were crisp and there was hardly a stain on the carpeting, which was an unusual greenish-brown color that certainly gave the building its own character that probably most who entered would have preferred to be forgotten in their short-term memory banks. Still, whoever owned the apartment complex took the time and effort to maintain a clean place to live, but could have splurged more on better sets of lights. The fluorescent lighting above washed out the colors of the carpeting, as if whatever touched its light was infected and stunk.

I knocked on Valery's door and was met with a gleaming face. She unhooked the chain lock and allowed me entrance. It was a breath of fresh air to be in her apartment. It was always much cleaner than my own, except today. It wasn't that it was dirty, compared to my apartment, nothing was, but it was a few grades lower than the baseline of tidy that she usually maintained.

"I'm sorry about the mess, I just haven't had much energy recently," she fretted, rushing around the kitchen to pile up the dishes in the sink and wiping the counters.

"It's fine, Val, don't worry about it," I assured her while I wandered over to the cabinet to find a clean glass, which I filled with water from the overstuffed sink now precariously filled with dirty dishes balancing upon each other. I opened another pantry door, in search of painkillers. I knew she had some; she always had medicine on hand. I noticed a bottle of pills that I hadn't seen before. It appeared mostly full and the label was glossy and new. Curious, I reached for it, but Valery spotted me.

"Those are mine," she warned. "What you're looking for are on the top shelf."

"What is this?" I asked, pointing to the new bottle.

"Medicine," she said, and I felt like she was embarrassed, so I quelled my curiosity, abandoning a barrage of concerned questions, and reached above it for the well-used bottle of painkillers. However, she offered more, though while avoiding my gaze. "I only need it sometimes, and when I take it, it doesn't help anyway. It doesn't make me feel like me."

Now that she'd opened the gate a bit wider, I felt comfortable to ask, "Help with what?"

Her dimples illuminated her face as she smiled. "It doesn't matter. You want any brownies to help wash those pills down?"

I sighed, recognizing indications of a stop sign. "Milk?" I asked.

She pulled a quart of milk from the fridge and handed it to me, along with a brownie.

I dug in and took swigs from the milk carton. Valery didn't drink milk. She only kept some for me, which just made me love her even more. Still exasperated from the state of her apartment, I washed the dishes, while she dried them. I was no detective, but I knew she was off and not acting herself, though I didn't think she would tell me more than she had already divulged. I wanted to ask her, figure it out, and fix it, but sometimes fixing wasn't the answer.

Using the scruffy side of the sponge, I pushed down with all of my might onto the pan and scraped as hard as I could against the black burn marks. With furious scrubbing, it still wouldn't pull off the pan.

In the corner of my eye, I saw her eyeing me as my frustration increased. "It's not coming off," I said. "It needs to soak."

"Oh, stop. Let me do it."

I raised my eyebrows at her. "What?" I asked incredulously. "Okay, be my guest!" I relinquished my soapy weapon and resorted to the damp rag she handed me instead.

Within a matter of seconds she exclaimed, "See? Just needs a bit of elbow grease," showing off a gleaming pan.

Apprehensive to her witch-like powers, I growled, "Well, guess I don't have greasy elbows."

She smiled and pointed at my dripping sleeves. "No, it looks like you have wet elbows, at least, but you'll get there!" She turned back to the dishes, but I let the damp dish towel hang. Engrossed in scrubbing more dishes, Valery didn't notice as I twirled the towel down to a fine point. Excess water from the towel splashed as the end whipped toward her, but I missed my target. She was too slow to react against a follow up whipping attempt. A squeal from Valery confirmed the hit. Giggling, she retaliated with splashing from the sink, but it wasn't enough to ease my barrage. Realizing her attempts were futile, she tried dodging around the kitchen, even using a cutting board as a shield, protecting her bottom. We raced around the apartment, making more of a mess, but we didn't care.

With a twist of her ankle, she slipped on a sofa cushion and crashed to the ground. All laughing immediately ceased and I dropped the towel. I raced to her. Kneeling down, I asked if she was all right and rolled her over. I saw a flash of dimples before she pulled me to her lips. She was safe, I was safe, and everything was perfect.

Dinner with the Devil

"Is that you, Boy?" My mother's familiar screech came down the hallway from the living room. I responded and took my shoes off at the door, placing them perfectly side by side. As I passed the cabinet in the hallway, I stopped.

The little figure of the boy in a raincoat with the eerie smile had been placed right up against the glass of the cabinet. Other figures, slightly behind him, had followed suit. Their conniving grins and tilted heads were closer than I liked. I had just rearranged them the other day, and yet there they were, so close to the glass that the figure of the boy in the raincoat would fall if someone opened the glass door.

I found the key, and twisted it into the lock. It popped, and I held my hand underneath to catch the boy in the raincoat. As I predicted, upon gingerly opening the glass door, the boy teetered and fell into my open palm. I apprehensively pushed the figures back into place, taking care to shove the boy with the raincoat all the way in the back, completely hidden behind the other figures.

"What's taking you so long, did you get lost or something?"

I rolled my eyes, locked the cabinet, and found

my mother in her rocking chair. "Did you move the figures in the hallway cabinet, Mom? I'm getting tired of moving them back into place."

"Oh my," she said with a sarcastic gasp and a hand flutter to her heart. "Such an accusatory tone!"

"So, is that a yes?"

"Jesus Christ, boy, do you think I give a shit what's in those damn cabinets? That was never my obsession, those figurines, but now apparently it's yours. I'm not surprised, you take after your father, and those things were his."

The night was starting out so well. I decided to rip the band aid off. "Valery is coming over here to have dinner with us tonight."

My mother blinked, and with a growl she said, "Who?"

"You've only met her one time, but I like this girl. We get along well, and I really want the two of you to get to know each other a bit better."

"… Is that so?"

"We've been together for a good while now, and we've already talked about getting married." Before my mother could interject, I added, "Just do me a favor and be on your best behavior."

I retreated into the kitchen before my mother could complain further. It wasn't long before I had fully prepared the casserole for dinner and the oven beeped, signaling it had preheated. I stuck the casserole dish into the oven and set a timer. It wouldn't be long before Valery rang the doorbell, so I checked on my mother, who was fast asleep in her chair.

I tiptoed backward, avoiding any unnecessary sounds that would wake her. Down the hallway I went, where I stopped to confirm the figures hadn't moved, and up the stairs to my mother's room. She never went up there anymore; she was too weak and she said many times previously that she preferred her chair, insisting it was more comfortable than any mattress she could afford on discount.

Dust had covered the room, except for the scuffed tracks on the wood floor leading to the bureau. I knew exactly where to look. Inside the topmost drawer was my mother's jewelry. Many of them were antiques, quite a few more were trash, but she didn't care about any of them anymore. I took a pearl necklace and a matching set of earrings, and slid them into my pocket. If they were real, they would sell for a good sum, allowing me to make up for the money I had lost gambling the previous night and maintain the lease to my apartment.

My mother hadn't worked in years, especially after her surgery. The health insurance company barely covered half the cost, and my job was simply not enough to pay for her mortgage, rent, and food. Sure, my father's pension from working at the county fire department helped, but it wasn't enough.

The doorbell rang. A sound that sparked a juxtaposition of excitement and foreboding.

I welcomed Valery at the door, and thanked her for the bottle of wine she had brought. I asked her to wait in the dining room while I escorted my grumbling mother to her seat at the table.

"Look, Mom," I said, trying to keep the atmosphere as light as possible for as long as possible, "Val brought some wine, would you like a glass?"

She snatched it from my hands and inspected the label. She crinkled her nose slightly, but said, "Yes, I suppose that'll do." Valery must have splurged on the bottle; my mother despised cheap wine. Either that, or she wasn't familiar with the type or brand. I briefly left them alone, which I hesitated to do, but quickly returned to the table with three glasses and a bottle opener. My mother and Valery had just started a conversation.

"I work as a bartender, fully trained and licensed."

My mother's eyebrows rose. "Is that so? That makes perfect sense."

Valery's cheeks flushed., "What do you mean?"

"Oh," My mother flicked her fingers nonchalantly, "It's just, well..." She looked at Valery up and down, "Must I really say it?"

Valery's cheeks became a darker shade of red as anger now replaced her earlier insecurity, "Yes, you do."

"Oh, fine then. Someone of your intelligence and body shape, I'm surprised you aren't working in a gentlemen's club. But good for you, bartending is a step up."

I had to cut in, "Mom, that's enough!"

"No!" Valery warned me, but then directed her attention back to my mother, "I'll have you know, I have a degree in engineering, but I believe in doing what you love for a living, so I choose to bartend."

"You chose to be a slave to the drunk masses over engineering?"

"I like mixing new drinks, discovering new tastes and concoctions. And the tips pay more than one might expect. I like speaking to new people; you can learn a lot from different people."

"With how you probably flaunt yourself, I have no doubt you rake it in. Boy, you best keep an eye on her or some man half as manly as you will take her away."

"Mother, that's enough!"

The oven beeped. The food was finished cooking. The two women glared at each other while I placed a hot plate in the center of the table.

Everyone's plates were filled, and my mother and I began to dig in. However, Valery gave the sign of the cross, gently tapping her forehead, chest, and either shoulder. I shot a glance at my mother. She noticed, but she kept her mouth shut; probably since food would spill out if she opened it. Just as I thought it was safe, my mother spoke, "I wouldn't have taken you for a Christian."

There was a tense silence, but Valery's dimples creased, "Oh? It's how I was raised."

My mother's eyebrows couldn't have raised any further, and she scanned over Valery's piercings and many assorted tattoos.

"Can you pass the salt?" Valery asked.

"What? My son's cooking not good enough for you? You have to go and tarnish it?" My mother said, glaring at Valery.

I sighed, reaching over to grab the salt, "Mom, you add salt to almost everything."

She huffed, "Yeah, but I'm your mother, I'm allowed to. And besides, the doctor told me I needed to eat more salt, he said it was good for my heart."

"What heart?" Valery said, and the room froze, each person waiting for another to breathe first. "You don't have a heart, and if you did, it's gushing black tar through your veins."

I stared, aghast, and my mother appeared to be frozen mid-bite.

"You are a fucking selfish, ungrateful ugly old

bitch. You've got nothing to live for anymore, so now you're just making everyone else's life miserable. Well not mine!" She shoved her plate across the table and knocked her chair over from standing so abruptly. She threw her napkin in my mother's face and said, "Shove that in your filthy face hole, you raggedy cunt," and stormed out.

I didn't know what to say. I had never seen Valery lose herself. I wanted to go after Valery, but something glued me to the chair. I cowered, waiting for my mother's reaction, but she gave no further indication of upset and resumed her bite, as if nothing had happened. She even snatched up the salt and dumped it over her food.

"I'm glad she had to leave dinner early, so we could have some time together without her looming over us." My mother took another bite as I tried to figure out why she wasn't livid about Valery's exit. She probably didn't want to give Valery the satisfaction. My mother finished chewing and poked her fork at me, gesturing like a devil with his pitchfork, "I'm telling you, there's just something off about her, I just don't like her."

"You could have tried to be nice."

"I love you too much to do that."
"What does that mean?!" I said flabbergasted.

"She's not good for you. She's phony, she's not

real. You are a kind, sweet man. You deserve someone equally kind, someone who would take care of you when you get old and weak as you do for me."

I clung to my anger, my mother deserved my wrath, but it was falling between my fingers like sand. I dug for more, but my mother's kind words seemed to spill the sand even more. She never spoke to me like that. Was she thanking me? Was she actually caring for once? But then the sand became wet, and I could grasp it within my fists again. She was only playing me, and she knew the best way to manipulate me.

"No," I said out loud to myself. "No," now directed to her, "you can't do that, not anymore. I'm not going to listen to your conniving words. I love Val, and she's not going anywhere." I stood abruptly, "But I am. From now on, you need to walk yourself to the kitchen, make your own food, and get your own goddamn salt."

My mother's hand shot out to my wrist, but her touch was delicate, not harsh like I expected after my outburst. She made a soft face that I had not seen in years. She looked like my mother again and she whispered, "No one will love you like I can."

Street Lights

The wind's speed had heightened since earlier, piercing through my coat like thousands of tiny daggers. Leaves pelted the streets, and I was the only person in sight. Valery was gone; far gone. She lived several blocks past my place from my mother's, so I had to backtrack toward my neighborhood. Her place was in a better lit residential area, with newer apartment buildings. Normal people, not old hobos on top of stacks of tires, walked the streets, and cars drove on well-kept asphalt. It was amazing how just five or six blocks away, a slathered junk of a neighborhood existed... my neighborhood. The closer I got to Valery and her apartment, the farther away I got from my cracked and broken neighborhood. Things were simpler with her. I could see more clearly when she was around, as if, without her, my head was caked in viscous sludge, then almost miraculously, like a drug, she unclogged and drained the ooze.

I pulled my coat around me. Though the wind gusts were loud, howling its rage in my ears, I could hear a distant church bell chime. Normally a welcoming tone to breach the harsh air, a dose of warmth where a safe haven waited in the distance; tonight, however, the church bell seemed faint and miserably unreachable. It toyed with me, and my mind drifted to the hospital with Isabel and Brian. They had acted so strangely... yet I couldn't help but wonder if their actions had any, even the slightest, value.... No, they were crazy. There was nothing there; they saw nothing. The world wouldn't allow it. The world was ruled by the intricacies of physics and science, not by crazy schizophrenic people and metaphysical nonsense... unless they knew something we didn't. What if they saw things that normal people could not? Their brains worked differently, insufficient in some areas, but heightened in other areas that allowed them to welcome and embrace the metaphysical anomalies of the world, as well as heaven, even hell.

Isabel's paranoia of people poisoning or sticking their genitalia in food was nonsense. She, like Brian and all the other patients, possessed little credibility; whatever they said or would say would be an incarnation of their damaged minds, nothing else. Isabel's strange trance was just another sign that her pills were not working correctly, and either they needed to raise the dosage or swap them for a new brand. And, back at the club, there was no way what I saw happened. Val was right. Obviously, I drank too much. I wasn't paying attention to how many I had that night, and some asshole probably slipped something in my drink. A silly mistake of not being vigilant enough.

I clung to my rationalizations. But the night seemed to squeeze me, press at my pressure points. And, despite my efforts in keeping the thoughts at bay, a torrential of puerile worry bullied its way in. Brian claimed he had something on him, and then whatever it was had fixed its attention to me. Wondering if it lingered behind me, I resisted the urge to touch my shoulders and back, but my mind whirled, my lungs caved, and I thought I would die if I did not check immediately. I reached a stiff inflexible arm around and checked. Nothing.

Of course there was nothing, what the fuck was I thinking? Why am I letting a man, hospitalized for his insanity, wreak havoc on my psyche and allow childish manifestations of fright? A question answered, but maybe there was actually something there.

I slapped my cheek. Now it burned twice as much, thanks to the wind.

Isabel, with her strained neck and bulging eyeballs, sniffing around me.

I slapped the other cheek.

"WRONG WAY!" I jumped in dismay, rolling on my ankle as I landed, and cursed, kicking at the crumbled asphalt. It was only the homeless man on the rubber tires. "Fuck you!" I shouted. "Go home to whatever shit cardboard box you sleep in. Why are you even here!?"

The homeless man slowly hobbled off his rubber throne as I waited for an answer. Without warning, his pace quickened and he was almost upon me. I could see his pupils, even through the dark. "I'm watching," he moaned like a bullfrog. "I'm watching out for you. Don't go." He pointed behind him, where he always pointed, and leaned in close to my face, his foggy breath billowing into my eyes, making them water. "Go that way. Choose the right way."

"Jesus Christ," I snapped, pulling away from him. "Go that way yourself, nutjob. Better yet, go get some help, because you plainly need it!" I turned away from him and plunged down the road with new vigor. I heard him mutter one last thing behind me, but the wind's roar drowned it out.

After a few more blocks, I turned the corner, and was now two blocks away from Valery's building. I double checked the street sign, confirming I was on the right road. It was pleasant to be on a street filled with numerous street lamps that actually provided decent light, guiding the way. I didn't feel too uncomfortable in my neighborhood, given the misery that clung to it; in this neighborhood I could relax. I hadn't realized how tense my shoulders had felt. I eased them down, relieving stress on my spine.

The street lights were prematurely decorated with garland and multicolored holiday lights, but I didn't mind. A shot of cheer was welcome while cleaning the wake of ashes left from the dinner from hell.

I finally reached Valery's building. To my immense displeasure, the cold was now fully acquainted with the inside of my coat, but that was the furthest from my mind. In front of me, past the fence line that bordered Valery's building, was a small park, fitted with benches and winding pathways. Well-trimmed grass with cold, bleached tips were littered with dead leaves.

All of this was well and good. Except the park was where Valery's building should have been, and there was no building in sight.

I reeled backward, double checking my surroundings. I craned my neck up to the street signs that confirmed I was in the right place. The coffee shop across the street was boiling with people; cupping their steaming beverages, they crossed the street to the park to join the other jolly patrons for a rest on the benches. Relentlessly, I checked the street name on a sign again. This *was* the spot. This was where I had been the other day to drop off the eggs at Valery's apartment, this was where we spent time getting ready for dinner only hours before. *This* was where it should be, and yet, it wasn't. I searched around frantically for some clue, something; anything I could not recognize to know I was in the wrong place. But I couldn't. Everything I saw on the street was exactly as I had remembered.

I found a couple of patrons, clutching their coffee cups, and asked, "Was there a building here? How old is this park?"

One of them, a young man with a full, well-kept beard gave an apprehensive response, "Nope, that park's been here since I've lived around here; just over three years now." He tried to walk on, but I stopped him. "Are you sure? There was an apartment building here just hours ago; no park. I was in it, room 301!"

"Sorry, man, can't help you." He walked past me to follow his friends, but I barred his way.

"I'm telling you," I said, "I was just in there, and it wasn't a goddamn park!"

In reaction, he gave me a swift shove, which I did not expect, and sent me sprawling. He seethed, "Get out of the way, nutjob!" He shook his head, looking down at me. As I picked myself up, he said, "Dude, you need help." Openmouthed, I stared after him while he went back to join his friends.

I clearly must have been mistaken. There *was* an apartment building, but I had just wandered down the wrong street. I decided to turn back around. It was cold, too cold to wander through the streets in search of her apartment. So, I pulled out my phone, which I noticed had a low battery, and dialed her number. It rang, too many times without an answer, so I hung up and called again. Finally, I heard a voice on the other end of the line, but it was not Valery's voice. I couldn't hide the distress in my voice when I asked for Valery, but the woman, whose voice I could not place but undoubtedly had heard before, said, "I am not Valery. Please do not call again." And then it dawned on me.

"Isabel? How did you get this number? Do you have Valery's phone?" But the line was cut from the other end. I redialed, but the phone wouldn't even ring. "Shit!" I slammed my phone shut, thrust it back into my pocket, and began to backtrack toward my apartment.

As I walked, I tried remembering what Isabel had said to me back in the hospital. She warned me about a bill. Cash was what I first thought of, but how could I ever worry about having too much money? I sure had plenty of bills to pay—electric, water, and rent... but assuredly that wasn't what she was alluding to. Stumped, I moved on, trying to remember what else she had said. She'd said, "Listen and learn." And though I could have punched myself for doing it, I heeded her words and abruptly stopped and listened. Of course, as I suspected, I only heard the rustle of leaves and the buzzing of the old street light looming above my head like a vexing, unwelcome guardian angel.

But then I closed my eyes and listened; really listened. I unclenched my muscles, opened myself to the wind, and let it in. I felt like I had been battling the wind all evening, and in finally submitting to it, I felt invulnerable. The wind, and all the cold it brought with it, was now a faint brush against my thoughts, allowing me to ignore its eager prodding, and focus on listening. I tilted my head up, feeling the heat of the street light.

There was shock and a burst above me. I shielded my eyes from the raining shards of glass and felt a jabbing pain tearing at the bare flesh of my raised hand. I was left in the dark, unable to see the damage that had been inflicted, so I cursed and went toward the next street light several meters away. As I entered the street light's outer rim, its light gradually became brighter and clearer, so I was able to discern the damage. My skin had been peeled back in four or five different places, revealing gaping muscles and tendons. My stomach rolled. I tried tugging the skin flaps back over the open wounds, but a gag reflex pinned my efforts and, ultimately, I settled with grasping my wounded hand with the other hand as tightly as I could.

I needed to get to a hospital. I wrapped my healthy hand across my abdomen to reach into my phone pocket. I fumbled with the buttons, pushing and holding the power button, but it wouldn't turn on. The battery must have died.

I glared up at the street light above. But my anger simmered, turning cold and white. The street light began to emit a low hum, not unlike the specific note that escaped from Brian's lips. The hum seemed to intensify. Still grasping at my injuries, I raised my arms up and plugged one of my ears with my wounded hand to stifle the now ear-splitting buzz. Not wishing for another light bulb to burst overhead, I stepped out from underneath. The buzzing went even higher, even as I stumbled away. It dug into my eardrums, and I wished it would rupture them, so I would be free of the digging knife in my ear, but then it stopped.

I looked behind me, and the light bulb, still intact, had gone out. I quickened my pace toward my apartment, warily staring at the next street light ahead. As I drew closer, I could hear that it, too, was buzzing. My breathing began to strain as the air seemed to bite my throat. I quickened my pace even more, still grasping my wounded hand, and the street light now only a few meters away buzzed even higher, and I knew it would see a similar fate as the previous two. I jogged ahead, pushing past the street light just before it went out, and, as if by instinct, I knew that if I didn't make it to the next street light before its light went out, something terrible would happen...

I sprinted, desperate now to reach the next buzzing street light. All the way down the street, each light buzzed, intensified, and went out, just after I went through its light rays and pushed past it. The last street light was before me, and my lungs felt paralyzed, unable to pull in the air that I desperately needed. The buzzing was too high, and the street light too far. I wasn't going to make it. The searing pain in my legs felt like a white hot iron had been strapped around them. My brain pushed them forward, but my legs faltered, wobbled, and I fell. My shoulder took the brunt of the force, sliding several feet forward, but not enough. I was still too far from the last street light. I had to get there before it was too late, before the humming peaked.

I began to crawl, inching my way forward. A few meters away, the street light screamed, reaching its limit; it was about to explode and I wouldn't make it. Calling what little strength I had left, I pushed my feet hard against the ground in one last effort to make it past the light... and made it! As I looked up at the street light, it's screaming subsided. I took a step back toward the light and deeply inhaled its safety cone of light. Then I felt a shove, my entire body being dragged by a sudden wave of intense wind. The street light creaked and groaned in its cement holding, and I held on to it with my injured arm wrapped around it and the steel wrapped within my other fist. The force of the wind pulling at me raked underneath me and sprung my feet and legs into the air. I clenched my eyes, focusing on holding on to the street light with all of my feeble might; my hand was weakening, failing me.

Just as quickly as it had barreled through, the wind ceased, and I came crashing back down on the broken asphalt.

Shards of Tea

A sudden spike of adrenaline allowed me to scramble to my feet. My lungs screamed for air, but I ignored them and held what little dregs of breath I had left. My hand was stuck in the shape of the street light. It took me a moment to realize that, of course, everything was fine. The light above me shone bright with everlasting tenacity and the localized tornado that had rushed through seemed to have left no damage in its wake. Once the realization of safety settled within me, I allowed myself to gulp as much oxygen as my lungs desired.

I still cupped my wrist to my chest; it didn't seem to hurt, but the adrenaline would soon wear off. I chuckled to myself, making my way down the road again. It was not uncommon for light fixtures to break in succession. Though I was no electrician, this notion, whether correct or not, soothed my mind, and I was able to reach my dilapidated apartment building without further hindrance. That is, until I found that the front entrance had been blocked with layers of plywood and sprawling paint reading "Indoor stairs under construction: use fire escape."

I gave an acidic stare at the shuttered door

before rounding the corner and pulling down the fire escape ladder with my good hand. I half expected the rusted metal to give under my weight and break at the hinges, but it was surprisingly secure as I climbed. I reached the emergency balcony and, out of the corner of my eye, I saw flickering. I turned, a wave of wind clawing at my eyes until they spilt tears, and I saw it: something black, cowering on top of the closest street light. I squinted my eyes, searching for detail. It looked like it had wings folded around itself, like some kind of large bird, but its body was far too enormous, with talons that gripped the light bulb. It opened its immense scaly wings while I clung against the railing, trying to get a closer look. Its gaze pierced my way, and I heard a familiar guttural hiss: *DO IT.* The light burst as it clenched its fists of talons upon take off.

"Hey!"

I whirled around to see Valery calling from the nearby window. My body flooded with relief at finding her back at my apartment, but the comfort was short lived. Knowing the creature was seconds away from piercing my skin, I dropped to my hands and knees, shielding my head from the inevitable onslaught.

But I felt nothing; nothing but the steel bars sinking their coldness through my layers of clothes. Only after Valery called out two more times was I able to peel back my hands from my head and push myself up. I searched around, but the creature was gone and the street light was empty.

Not wishing to stay outside any longer, I hopped through the window, slamming it shut behind me. Valery glided away toward the tiny kitchen and said, "I'll get us something warm to drink, you must be freezing."

Eager for a moment's rest, I slumped down on my bed. Though my body lay still, my mind was racing. The people at the hospital were trying to warn me this whole time. Isabel smelled it, and Brian saw it. I was a true believer now; I had to be; I saw it with my own eyes. What the fuck was that thing? Was I safe now that I was inside? I was compelled to jump out of bed and press my forehead against the window to stand watch. I cupped my hands around my eyes, to better discern the hell that assuredly peered at me with its haunting gaze somewhere from the dark. My efforts induced little peace of mind. While I could not see the creature out there, I knew it was watching me, from some unturned shadow, waiting to claw me in two.

I heard Valery's footsteps approaching the bedroom, so I frantically abandoned my search for the creature and resumed my earlier posture on the bed. She'd think I was crazy if I told her what I saw; anyone would think I was crazy if I told them what I saw.

Valery returned, holding out a steaming mug. I

felt safer now, cupping the mug for warmth. She took a sip from her own mug, then placed it on my bureau. She leaned against it with a sullen face, and said, "I'm sorry for tonight. I... She just struck a nerve, and I couldn't control my temper." I had so many questions about the creature, and my heart had barely begun to settle. I wished for a longer respite to gather my thoughts, and when I didn't say anything, she apologized a little louder, which finally forced me to respond, "She's an old bitch, don't worry about it."

"Baby, take a sip of your tea, is it okay? Do you need more sugar, because I could get some more—"

"No, it's fine," I said, after a large gulp, "thanks, Val."

I retreated back into my mind, thinking about the events of the night. I had to ask; no more ignoring everything.

"Val," I began, carefully articulating what I wanted to say, "after I left my mother's, I went to find you. Except, when I went down your street, your apartment building was gone. Instead, there was a park..." I waited, I wanted to see her reaction. Her face contorted into one of bewilderment. "Are you feeling alright?" Her words were not what I had hoped for.

Growing irritated, I said, "Yes, I'm fine, the park; your apartment—"

"I've been living with you for a long while now;

the park's been there for who knows how long. Baby, are you sure you are feeling well?"

How was that possible? I looked around, and I saw many of her clothes, mostly undergarments, strewn about.

"I don't know," I said. "I guess I've been seriously stressed out." I checked the clock by the bed. The club would be opening soon, but I had no intention of going back outside with that beast hanging around.

"Are you thinking of going back out?" she asked with concern in her voice.

I shook my head.

"What happened?" She kept probing, "It was something I said at dinner, wasn't it?" She stood, "That's it isn't it? I said I was sorry!"

"Christ! It wasn't about dinner! I just..." I needed to tell her, but I couldn't. I blurted out, "I went looking for you at your old apartment, and then felt like I was losing my mind when it wasn't there. I was distracted and worried when walking back and then... I was jumped on my way back home."

She gasped, sliding herself beside me on the bed. "Oh, baby, are you alright? Did it hurt you?"

I looked down at my wrist to survey the damage I had suffered from the street light. But the skin was smooth—perfect and intact. I stared at my veins, perfectly pumping blood through my body. I didn't know what to think. So I didn't think.

"No, I guess I'm fine."

She wrapped her arms around me. She was so warm. "How much did they take?"

"Nothing, it seems I was able to get away before anything could happen."

"I should call the police!"

But before she could leave the bed I exclaimed, "No! No, there's no point. I didn't get a good look at it—him I mean."

She came back to me, holding me again. "I'm so sorry." She breathed into my ear. "It's alright, you're safe now, with me." Her embrace tightened before she let go, reaching for her mug. "Drink, baby, it'll help." I consented. The tea gave an uncharacteristic tingle of enhanced warmth as it glided down my throat. She was right, it was making me much more relaxed and supple.

Valery's demeanor began to shift as her lips drifted toward my ear again. She whispered, "I can make you feel so much better... no one will love you like I do." I grunted in pain as she grabbed my crotch. Before I could tell her not to be so rough, she began to caress it instead.

"Val... Val!" I pushed her away, forcing her off the bed. "I'm not in the mood!"

She gave a quirky smile from above. "Is that so?" her eyes narrowed to my crotch. She was right, I had gotten hard, yet I felt little urge to do anything about it. "I don't want to do it right now, Val, just drop it."

"Oh?" she said, biting her lip. "Just drop it?" She turned away from me. I heard a shatter, and tea soaked the old carpet beneath her feet. "Oh... what have I done?" she said sarcastically, batting her eyelashes. She pushed her ass out, shaking it slightly as she bent to retrieve the broken bits. Distracted in her efforts to entice me, she gasped, recoiling slightly from a sharp piece that had snagged her finger. She turned her head towards me, licking drops of blood that were now dripping down her finger.

A mix of horror and awe forced me to keep my gaze. She crawled on her hands and knees, pieces of the mug gouging at her skin, until her palms were wet with red. She reached for my zipper, leaving a bloody mess over my pants. I pushed her away again, but she forced her way through, and dug out what she had been looking for. She wrapped her bloody hands around me, leaving blood smears before using her mouth to slurp it up. Though I was so hard it hurt, her attempts in pleasing me did not feel as they should have. Instead, it felt like I was face fucking a rose bush; beautiful, but tough and thorny. She pulled back to look up at me. I expected her green eyes, but a shocking set of orange bloodshot eyes bore into me instead. In my fright, I jumped, slamming my knee against the bottom of her jaw. "Shit! Sorry!

Fuck! Are you okay?" Her green eyes looked up at me, and she gave a bloody grin, reaching for me again.

"Stop," I said, apprehensively searching for any strange colors in her eyes, but they were normal again. "You're hurt."

She didn't care. She scoffed and pushed me onto the bed. She straddled me, pushing my arms up over my head, and kissed me. Hard. So hard, I could feel her teeth gouging my lips. I tasted blood, and I began to panic. I pushed against her, but she was far too strong. How could such a tiny person pin me down without any sign of effort? I pushed harder, and this time she released me. She tore off her clothes, ripping them with inhuman strength, and turned away from me on all fours. She shook her ass, inviting me in, and said, "Come on, baby, fuck me. Fuck me in the ass, you fucking bitch. You know you want to."

I refused. *What the fuck was wrong with her?* Neither one of us had spoken about trying it; in fact, I was sure we both had no intention of ever trying it. She slapped her own ass, leaving a bloody handprint, and a moan escaped her pierced lips. "Fuck me!" she demanded. "Fuck your woman like the whore that she is." After a pause, she said, "What? You aren't man enough to do it, huh?" She rolled her hips, and I gritted my teeth. The emasculation forced me forward, and I placed my palm over her hip; I wanted to fuck her, to show her, to punish her.

As I positioned myself, I saw a shadow on her bare shoulder. The tattoo on her shoulder molded, boiling on her skin. What used to be a raven transformed into a hunched creature, man-like yet indistinguishably a bird of prey. Black and enormous, with blazing orange eyes, a sharp crooked beak, and a face whose rotted flesh dripped from its skull.

My tip touched her, and she began to moan loudly. She clenched her own breast, pinched her nipple, and shrieked, *"DO IT!"*

I plunged, ripping through her. Her screams of agony and pleasure intensified my thrusting. I pushed as hard as I could, reaching deep into her, resulting in further screams of pain and euphoria. She reached down from the bed and retrieved a shard of the mug. She placed it on the outer part of her thigh and dug. Black liquid spilled from the wound, but her moans only intensified. I pulled out. I couldn't go on; everything had gone too far.

"Put it back in! *DO IT!*" she screeched, plunging the shard into her vagina. I tried backing away, but my muscles were frozen, incapacitated from the shock. She twisted and jabbed the shard inside herself with a moan of ecstasy, then yanked it out, releasing a river of black from her vulva that spilled and splattered over the mattress. Directing her attention to me, she said, her voice deep, distorted, and garbled, "Baby." It started like her voice, but it became even more distorted and deeper. "Where are you going? I need you, baby." She brandished the shard. "No one will love you like I can."

She lunged.

Patience

The alarm went off. A familiar sound, I had grown so used to it by now, I could have easily ignored it and fallen back to sleep. My eyelids fluttered open slightly, just to confirm the time. But I was no longer in my apartment. I sat up with my elbow resting on the cotton rock that served as a pillow. I was lying on a white twin bed, with white sheets and matching white blanket. The walls were white, except for a few un-interesting paintings taped at the corners. There was a window, but it was barred, and underneath was a dusty heating vent. There was a small desk in the corner, coupled with a chair the size a child would use. There was no doubt I was in a room at St. Elizabeth's.

Remembering what had happened, I seized my crotch, and found it was safe though sore. I examined the bandage wrapped around my throbbing wrist. My mind's eye remembered the flapping dangling skin pieces. I thought to unravel it to see the damage; instead, I leaned back into the pillow, sighing deeply—but my mind splintered to those orange, bloodshot eyes. Those eyes...

The alarm system went off again, but since I was more awake, I realized it was more of a buzzer. I fumbled with the sheets and blankets, my bandaged hand getting in the way, and clambered to the door. It wouldn't open. I pulled and shoved, but it wouldn't budge.

I had been in this position before. One time, during my first few weeks working at the hospital, I'd accidentally got locked in one of the patient's rooms while I was cleaning it. Someone had come down the hallway and had locked it along with the others for that night. Despite my hollering, I wasn't found until an hour later. It appeared that, once again, I was in a similar position. But luckily, this time I heard footsteps down the hallway, and I eagerly waited at the door. I caught the attention of the nurse who walked by. Through the bars, I saw that she had her black hair, blazed with streaks of grey in a bun.

"Excuse me!" I said. She stopped and peered into my room, "Hi, I think someone locked this on accident. I need to get out of here."

"Of course you want to get out. Here, just give me a moment, and I will unlock it for you..." She fumbled in her pockets, and that was when it hit me. She had a familiar face, yet it was so distinctly different; refined.

"Isabel?" I asked. She was well kept, her hair perfectly placed in a bun without any frizzing or loose strands, and her makeup immaculate without any splotches or globs.

"Yes, darling, I'm sorry you are still stuck in here. Someone was supposed to get you earlier, Dr. Lancaster would like a word with you."

She had discarded her long hippy dress for one of the nurse's outfits. But her choice of clothing wasn't the strangest thing about my encounter with her, it was that she seemed completely sane. She spoke without her usual paranoia, her nostrils remained normal and unflared, and her eyeballs were safely stuck inside their sockets where they belonged. The stark difference in her appearance, and how she held herself, shocked me. "Isabel, you're looking great today; do they have you on a different medication?"

"That's none of your business," she snapped. "And don't think I don't know what you're up to. What you've been doing with Miss Malim, it's not right." She started to stalk away, but turned around and curtly told me to follow her. She began to escort me down the hallway, as if I didn't know the way. I wondered what she meant by Miss Malim, but I felt I shouldn't press the notion any further, considering her disdain on the matter.

Several patients and personnel were meandering the hallway, peering out the windows, speaking to one another, or simply staring into space, without caring who gave them an incredulous glance as they lurked about. A man in a wheelchair, positioned facing the windows, stared outward toward the world as if he had lost everything he loved and cared for. His attention shifted, and his head rolled on his neck toward me. He stared at me as I followed Isabel, the sorrow in his eyes remaining; they were glassy and shone with despair.

I tried to keep my eyes locked forward to ignore his tenacious gaze, but suddenly, he lunged outward, clawing at the hem of my pants. "Go back! You can't be here. Face it! FACE IT! If you don't face it, it will take what you hold most dear. I wasn't there and I lost her here, there, and everywhere. FACE IT!"

I tried to pull my ankle away, but his grip was too tight. "That's how she died. She's gone because of ME! BECAUSE OF ME!"

I finally regained control of my extremity, thanks to Isabel forcing the man away and back into his wheelchair. He gave me one last look before snapping back into his catatonic state like a flame snuffed out with one forceful blow. Now he sat completely still and dead-eyed, looking through the window into oblivion.

I veered off Isabel's course. I gave a cautious step toward a familiar man by one of the barred windows. It was the perfectly groomed bearded man from the coffee shop near Valery's, except he was no longer perfectly groomed. His beard and hair were wild, and his horn-rimmed glasses were scuffed, brittle, scratched, and slightly askew. He sat motionless, muttering with vapid eyes, "Elephants grow in the fields at night; the heaven's picnic is picturing itself within a balloon; a mighty balloon that's full of hair. I'm waiting to be eaten, I want to feel warm and let the acid seep into my skin, just like coffee at the park. I wonder where the elves sleep, and what the pencil's lead says when his tip breaks from furious writing."

I waved my hand over his face, trying to catch his attention, and with a significant delay, his eyes lazily focused on mine. Though his eyes were directed my way, his focus was shallow, as if he saw through me to the opposite wall. I tried speaking to him, asking him what had happened to him between the other night and now. However, after a long pause where I expected him to respond, his eyes veered off again and he resumed his erratic muttering. Before I could press him further, Isabel came up from behind, saying, "Come, you should leave him be. He is not well, and asking too many questions will only make things worse and make him more aggravated." She pulled me away.

"Follow me, Dr. Lancaster is eager to speak with you," she repeated. "We'll have to go through the main room, please stay close and do not wander off again." She said it pleasantly, but I knew if I did not heed her this time, she would become even more irritated than she already was. I followed her, wondering who Dr.

Lancaster was, and investigating my surroundings with wide eyes and bewilderment. Was I dreaming? I had to be. People from my life were sprinkled in this dream. They looked and appeared as themselves, but were far from themselves.

I was in ward 2B. I knew it well. The architectural layout was exactly the same as it was in real life. There was one long hallway filled with rooms for patients on one side, and rows of barred windows on the other side. A shorter hallway bisecting the hallway with the rooms led to the main room where most of the day's events unfolded. While the layout was identical, the people, tables, benches, fake plants, and even the lighting was different. It seemed brighter, almost clearer, as if I could see farther down the long hallway with more precision.

I doggedly followed Isabel through the main room, catching glimpses of people sitting at tables, playing board and card games with each other. A nurse I thought I recognized strolled through the array of tables and chairs, offering patients something to drink from a trolley she pushed. She wasn't facing me, so I veered off course to approach her, but any angle I tried, I could not see her face. It was as if looking in multiple mirrors where the eyesight angles were so contorted that I could not position myself in the perfect line. "We're almost there," Isabel interjected, pulling me away.

We passed a man, who I recognized as Brian, standing guard at the exit of the main area. I expressed my enthusiasm in recognizing him, but his face remained deep in thought as he looked down at me. I didn't realize how tall he was when I was helping him through his traumatic breakdown, but there he was, completely lucid and fully in control of his mental and motor skills. He allowed Isabel and me entrance, but I remained silent as we passed him. I wanted to greet him as I would any other patient, but it seemed out of place...

Isabel and I rounded a corner, and she rapped on a door with Dr. Lancaster's name etched into the marbled glass. There was a gruff answer, and Isabel nodded for me to enter. I proceeded with my ritual and entered. I noticed Isabel giving me a sympathetic smile.

I stared at him, my eyes glued to the familiar face. I couldn't believe it. This was going way too fucking far. Someone was trying to play a prank—a good prank. Whoever was behind it certainly did not pull any punches. Dr. Lancaster cast a smile. "It's good to see you lucid and back in reality. Sit down." Reality? Lucid? What the fuck?

"Sit down," Dr. Lancaster repeated. I didn't; I was too agitated. A maniacal laugh escaped from me, and I said, "The last time I saw you, you were, as usual, on top of some old banged up car tires shouting and hollering at me." The man, whom I had known for many months now as the hobo I frequently ran into on the streets, nodded his understanding. His hair now was closely barbered, allowing for the baldness on the top of his head to be more distinguishable. His beard, though still long, was managed, clean, and brushed. A pair of small circular spectacles donned the lower part of his nose. "Yes, yes, so you have said. When was this? When did you see me last?"

"Uh, last night," I said, still shocked at how well-groomed he had suddenly become.

"I see.... It seems you've had a small relapse of sorts. Sometimes missing just one dose can do that. How else have you been feeling?"

"This is a joke, isn't it?" I said, raising my voice. "Who is doing this to me? Who paid you to go to the barbershop and give you a lab coat costume?" I was on the verge of exploding. "Because it's not funny anymore! Come on out!" I called out and swiped at the fake plant in the corner expecting someone to be hidden there. "Clearly this isn't a dream, because it's way too real. So, it must be a joke. I know you're out there, just come out, you've got me! Real hilarious. That's enough, I'm done!"

Dr. Lancaster stood, his brow dark, and pointed to the seat opposing his desk. His silence frightened me into equal silence, and I understood that what was happening was indeed happening to me, whether it was real or not, and I needed to understand the ramifications. I silently filled the chair while he resumed his seat and returned to his earlier tranquilness. My eyes wandered over the room. Multiple accolades demonstrating his prowess in psychology and wellness peered over the shelves or were nailed to the walls. Still, one trophy, on the shelf above Dr. Lancaster's head, stood out among the rest; it didn't fit the medical mold. It was a gold racing trophy with a stack of tires. On top was a majestic figure holding a flag.

"Yes, you always fixate on that one," Dr. Lancaster said, tracking my eyeline, and sighed, as if tired of a worn routine. "What is it?" I asked, transfixed on the triumphant figure on top of the tires. "Just an old memento of my younger, wilder days," Dr. Lancaster explained before pressing on.

The fluorescent lights were peaked, making Dr. Lancaster's skin look like aged greenish plaster. "I assure you, this is no joke," he said in a voice level and calm, "nor is it a dream, but I think you've already figured that one out for yourself. You need to tell me the truth. Have you been taking your pills—your medicine?"

"Pills? No, I haven't, I don't take any medicine."

His face was of dismissive disappointment. "… I see, I'm sure just a lapse in your memory. We'll have Nurse Malim ensure you are taking your pills." He leaned in, eyes locked into mine, and said, "It is imperative you take your medication. Do you understand? You need to follow my instructions and do as I suggest. The nurses and I are worried about you, but if you listen to us, no harm will come to you, and you will start to feel even better than you do now. You being here with me right now is already a sign that the new medication has made an impact and you are on your way."

His sticky, honey-colored eyes bore through mine, so I looked at the ceiling instead, but nodded my understanding. I had no recollection of any kind of medication. Everything was different, and out of sorts. I was stuck, and all I could do was follow the path and see where it led.

Defeated, I asked, "Where am I?"

"You are in St. Elizabeth's Mental Hospital."

"I know *where* I am," I snapped. "I work here. Everything is the same, but different. This isn't your office, it's actually a medical storage room locked by a key card. I've been here hundreds of times... but not *here* here. You shouldn't be *here*."

"On the contrary, I should, and so should you. I've said this before, but I hope you'll take it in this time: You don't work here in St. Elizabeth's. In fact, you've never worked here. I know this will come as a shock, but stay calm, you are in a safe place. We wouldn't want you to hurt yourself again," He pointed to my bandaged hand. I pulled it off the desk, hiding it from his view in embarrassment. "What we do here at St. Elizabeth's is not easy, but it's necessary. Many challenged folks find themselves here, whether they were admitted by family, or brought in... by other means. We aim to give the best care we can provide, but you have to follow the rules. You cannot hurt yourself anymore, or we will have to start certain measures to assure it will not happen again, do I make myself clear? Do I?" I nodded in reply. "Good." He leaned back into his chair. "Now, do you have any questions for me?"

I wondered what I should tell him. The voice in my head urged me to say nothing. If I spoke the truth, and told Dr. Lancaster about the creature or Valery... she was the last thing I could remember before waking up, those fiery orange eyes.

"Anything?" Dr. Lancaster asked, knowingly interjecting my thoughts. I shook my head, but he looked displeased as if he expected me to indulge him. "I see.... In that case, please return to the main room. They will be handing out medications to patients within a half hour. Wait there, and Nurse Malim will ensure you take your pills. Remember," he tapped his computer screen, "we're watching, we'll know if you take your pills or not."

I left Dr. Lancaster's office without another

word. Brian was waiting for me on the other side. "Follow me. Patients aren't allowed without an escort in this section." I forced a nod. I didn't like being called patient. I was no patient. I was as sane as they were! I needed answers, and Dr. Lancaster wouldn't give them to me. This was my chance. "Brian?" I asked, "You remember, don't you? I helped you out of that trance you had, remember? The one where you saw that creature? You were right! It's real!"

"Calm down. No funny business."

"I saw the creature!"

He gritted his teeth "You best calm down." He rolled his sleeves menacingly. I lowered my voice, but still pressed him. "Don't you remember?"

"No. You're not well. Nurse Malim will be making the rounds in the main room soon." He shooed me forward, and resumed his post surveying the main room by the door that led to Dr. Lancaster's office.

Though the room was full, I felt lost and alone. No one was listening to me. The people I recognized were not acting themselves. They had familiar features, but alien personalities. They were nothing like what I remembered.

I surveyed the room, looking for a place to wait. A box television hung in a corner, running quietly, but it was being ignored by the patients. People of many adult ages sat on old olive-colored sofas, while others sat around tables in scrappy orange cafeteria chairs. They hunched over the tables, conversing with each other. I spotted an open seat by a table full of patients playing cards, the comfort of playing cards drawing me in.

Not knowing how to introduce myself, I simply asked, "Is there room for one more?"

They peered up at me, suspicion looming in their eyes. They looked to one person at the table for guidance. He was a dashing man, dressed like the rest of the patients, but he wore a red napkin around his neck like a handkerchief, separating himself from the rest of the crowd. "Howdy, partner. Take a seat, we have room." The others at the table eased their blocky shoulders. "What you got?"

I blinked. "What?" It took me a second to realize what he meant. "To bet?" I asked.

"Yes for betting! What do you got in your pockets?"

I checked my pockets. They were empty. "I don't have anything."

"That's fine. We buy in with what we can. What do you have that none of us have?"

I shrugged. It looked as if I would have to stand in front of the abandoned television instead. "Some of us use extra crackers from our meals, others go all out and bet entire meals or drinks. Danny over here somehow has collected nurse's buttons—a high commodity at the table right now. Do you have any nurse buttons?" I shook my head.

"You take pills?" He snorted. "Trick question, here we all do. I'll tell you what. You can play a hand, but your buy-in for the hand will be your water. You know, the little cup the nurse gives to us to drink with the pills. If you lose, you gotta suck the pills down dry, and the winner gets your water. We can play like that until you make something of yourself. What do you say, partner?"

I nodded, and the round began. As he dealt, he said, "The name's Harvey, William Harvey. This here is Danny, and on your left is Ray."

Danny seemed normal, just like Harvey, but Ray's eyes bugged and bulged outwards. I couldn't tell if he was looking at me, my cards, his cards, or out the barred window behind Harvey. I pulled my cards close to me and restrained a grin. I had an ace and a jack, both in the suit of clubs. The odds were in my favor. I eagerly waited as the others bet their lunch scraps. Harvey dealt three more cards. The cards were all low numbers and suits of red, terminating my potential for a flush. My odds were thinning. I expected more from the next three cards, but all hope wasn't lost. All I needed to win was a single jack or an ace. I contained my contempt when the next card showed a king.

"King King King!" Danny stood up from his

chair. "Look, it looks like me, I'm King Daniel. I want to be a king."

The others didn't react like I did to Danny's exclamation, but Harvey said in a calm tone, "Sit back down, Danny, just play the game."

Reverting back to the cards, I couldn't back out; folding was not an option since I wouldn't accept defeat and would have little else to give on the next hand. All I could do was hope. With bandaged fingertips, Harvey pulled the next card out and revealed another king. This time, Danny began to hoot and holler even more about kings. The odds of one of these nutcrackers having another king was low, but then again, Danny had no poker face. My ace high could readily win the hand if luck was on my side...

"Alright, Danny, go ahead, show us what you got there, partner."

Danny dropped his cards and shouted, "Kings kings kings!" But all he had was a three of clubs and nine of diamonds. Ray revealed his hand. He had a pair of fours. I had already lost, but Harvey was hiding pocket queens.

"YEEHAW!" Harvey slammed his fist on the table, bouncing the cards a fraction off the surface, "The pot is mine! Oh," he looked at me, "and when that frisky nurse comes around, you owe me your water."

I sighed. I was never good at taking pills; fuck

all without water.

Just as I stood to leave, Harvey stood and offered a hand. A hand with a missing finger. "Good game, partner." He leaned in, gripping my hand with quiet aggression. "Keep quiet about all this. Gambling is frowned upon here. Don't be a rat." His tone polarized into jeering. "Looking forward to the next time, I always like extra water when taking my pills; makes it go down so much easier... I like making the nurses happy."

I gritted my teeth, but felt Brian's eyes boring into the back of my head. They were watching. I didn't like being watched. I needed to leave. If this was a dream, I was stuck in bed unable to wake myself up. I felt my desperation rise. None of this was real. I needed to get back to reality. Leaving this dreadful prison was the first step in making that happen. The emergency exit sign loomed near Brian's shoulder. An arrow pointed to the corner of the room and my eyes found the door. It was my best and only option. My eyes went back to Brian, who was big, but I was faster. If I could reach the doorknob I could easily outrun him down the stairs and out onto the streets.

I shifted my weight, waiting for a window of opportunity. The hands on the clock by the television steadily inched forward, but my desperation increased exponentially. My compulsion was driving my brain; all I cared about was exiting through that door to be free.

My body could not take the torment any longer; if I waited a second more I would have exploded. I lunged forward two steps, but on the third, I felt my foot slip underneath me. My other limbs waved wildly, but the fall was too quick. My teeth gouged into my upper lip and my brain sloshed in my skull. I rolled over, tasting blood, and caught a glimpse of what I had slipped on. With benign innocence, a white cowboy hat lay crumpled a foot away from my feet.

Reasoning with Madness

I awoke in the staff lounge. My nagging pager was buzzing. In the midst of my dozy wakefulness, I felt like an empty husk. I merely existed and nothing more. I felt no pain or worry. But then I blinked. It felt like my upper lip was three times its normal size, my shoulders sagged, and my temples pulsed like thunder.

Returning to reality from that horrible dream, I unclipped my pager, which demanded me to report to sector 2B. With sluggish resolve, I made my way out of the empty lounge and down the familiar hallways that led to sector 2B.

I walked past the storage room, but my dream, still fresh in my mind, made me turn back. I studied the door. The tag confirmed it was still a storage room and not the office of a Dr. Lancaster. I snickered in relief, and moved on toward the main room. The woman at the front desk pointed me toward the television. Standing on the sofa, eyes pinned to the television, was the hobo who stood on the tires in the street, also known as Dr. Lancaster.

I approached him, but his eyes were still glued to the television. Though I had not expected to see him, I was not surprised that one day or another, he would wind up in St. Elizabeth's.

"Come down from the sofa," I said, shaking my head at him. But I made sure to say it with kindness, which I had never given him before. He always had to be on top of something. "Do you have a room yet? Has anyone helped you?"

He trembled slightly on the sofa, the plush cushion rocking his knees. "Seeing is believing, isn't it?" he said with his hoarse voice and his eyes still glued to the television.

"That's what they say," I said, wondering how often he had come across a television. "Come down, and I'll show you to a room."

He blanched, and teetered on the sofa. "I know you." He pointed a knotted finger at me. "Did you go where I told you to go? Did you?! Did you take your medicine?"

I'd tried calming him down. The other nurses and patients were staring. Next, I pulled him away, silencing him with a shush. We went down the hallway toward the rooms to seek a little more privacy. Only the catatonic man in a wheelchair inhabited the hallway, someone else who I had previously ignored for so long. After the terrifying moment in my dream where he attacked me, I kept a wary eye on him. As we drew closer, and away from the main patient lobby area, I recognized the wheelchair man from earlier. I had noticed him before, but never stopped to think about how he had *always* been there, ever since I started working at St. Elizabeth's. He was never in a different spot, and it seemed he needed little attention from the staff. It was like he was part of the furniture, part of the hospital.

I was yanked away from my thoughts when the hobo Dr. Lancaster said, "You're like me, you see things. What do you see?" His eyes bulged, much like Isabel's had when she sniffed me in the hallway.

I couldn't contain my irritation. "I see you. A goddamn hobo that keeps following me around! Why are you here?"

He shook his head irritably, ignoring me completely. "I'm just like you. Like a lot of people. We see things. What things have you *seen*? I see things. Bad, awful, dark things. Sweet, light things too, but the black has a way of taking over the light."

My irritation dissipated slightly in interest. Could he be speaking of the creature I saw? I had no inclination whether or not confessing to the hobo was worth my time. He was a crazed lunatic who, instead of finding a job, made his career choice in stalking me. But the creature could still be waiting. As soon as I set foot outside after my shift, it might be after me again. I desperately needed information. And if this shifty hobo was willing to give it, I should be open to receiving it. I scratched my arm, itching with tenacity, but it didn't seem to relieve me much. My movements gave me away.

"What happened?" he asked, pointing to my injured hand. My bandage had fallen off when I had forcibly escorted him down the hallway, but what was truly puzzling—no, frightening—was that my wounds I thought I had suffered the other night had suddenly manifested again overnight, when it seemed earlier during the encounter of its origin I hadn't been injured enough to break the skin. Whatever the case may be, my skin around the wounds had grown red and purple, and they were oozing yellow pus.

"Got cut by some glass," I said, finally able to muster some sort of answer amidst my confusion. I tried to hide my hand behind my back, but he lunged and squeezed my arm forward to his eye level. He peered down at the wounds. "You didn't get that from glass."

His face grew grim, and his earlier hyper energy waned, giving him more of a wiser aura than before. I listened to him intently. "I've seen things all my life, things you wouldn't believe; things most would not believe; things they cannot see. So tell me, what have *you* seen?"

Perhaps the wise Dr. Lancaster lurked beneath this drab man. The grime and rags were a facade, seen by all who didn't bother to look closer. Just like I hadn't bothered. Maybe after all this time seeing him on the street, he could help me as he had claimed so many times before. I decided to describe the creature. But I could not tell him what had happened with Valery. Some things were best kept unsaid.

"I see..." My mind's eye flashed again to Dr. Lancaster. The homeless man before me, a trifle of what Dr. Lancaster had been, seemed saner than I had ever seen him on the streets. "I thought I saw it, too. It's a master hider, that's why I can't be completely sure. It hides in plain sight. It hides on the inside," he touched his belly, "and out." He leaned in closer to me, whispering, "But I do know this: Once it's found you, it won't leave until it gets what it wants."

"What does it want?"

Dr. Lancaster shrugged but his face was drenched in fear. "My guess? You. And after you, it'll come for me. When we start to believe... believe in it, it comes for you. It doesn't want to be known. It will follow you everywhere, you can't shake it off, and for those around you who don't see it... well they don't believe the pain and dread that you feel. One way or another, somehow, it is always watching... it doesn't matter where you go, what you do, it knows, and, somewhere, it watches." He leaned back, looking about the hallway. "It watches, even now."

Psychotropics

The rest of my shift was normal. Throughout it all I could think about was trying to get a moment with Isabel and Brian, but both were beyond intelligible. Their mental statuses had diminished significantly; they were undergoing increased dosages of their medications and needed to be quarantined in their room under full surveillance until the acute side effects from the higher dosages wore off. The nurses in charge of their well-being refused to let me see them, saying that they were not in the right mind. In a few days, perhaps, their bodies would acclimate to the new drugs and they would be able to shed more light on my situation. Before, I had barely listened to them, they were completely mad at the time, but now I saw that there was some merit in what they said. I was beginning to think that they were the sanest people I knew; only with them could I find answers. If not answers, then solace in the knowledge that they understood what I was going through.

At the end of my shift, I opened the exit door, once, twice, and three times, but hesitated on the fourth. I didn't want to go outside. What if that thing was waiting for me again? What if it was hovering above the awning, just waiting to pounce down and slice through me? I was lucky the last time. My ignorance saved me, but now I knew what was there, lurking and watching. The homeless Dr. Lancaster said it was always watching. It watched me now as I hesitated to leave the safety and warmth of St. Elizabeth's.

Brian's voice popped in my head. "You should have these. You need them. It is only focused on you now."

I dove into my pocket and withdrew the sunglasses he had given me. Without hesitation I put them on. A wave of warmth and safety came over me and I was able to make the first step toward my mother's house. What the sunglasses could offer in protection, I could not fathom, but did not squander the potential they had.

I was surprised when nothing happened. The air was cold, but the wind was calm. My neck and shoulders ached from shifting my head to look all around me as I walked, but the creature did not attack or appear. The roads were worse than I remembered, though. Cracks webbed through the pavement; some leading to potholes and some verging on sinkholes, but I was careful not to fall in.

I unlocked the front door, concluded my ritual, and embraced the warm... cold? I expected a warming sensation from the heater as I entered the house, but instead a wave of freezing air, colder than outside, broadsided me and left my lungs partially paralyzed. The hall was dark, except for a crack of light underneath the door leading to the living room and kitchen. I tried flicking on the light switch. I cursed; the light bulb was out again. I had changed it within the last week, and yet it had already burned out. But as I continued toward the door, my pace began to slow as I realized I was not alone in the dark hallway. A silhouette of a figure blocked my way near the figurine glass cabinet. My first instinct was to cry out in dismay, but I couldn't breathe in enough cold air. Without moving a step further, I used my peripheral vision, hoping to catch a more detailed view.

The light in the glass cabinet flicked on. Weak fluorescent light gave enough light to spotlight the figurines, but also gave me a better visual of who was before me. "Jane?" My older sister had her hands in the glass cabinet, moving the figurines from where I had placed them earlier. I moved closer, gaining more detail. She was naked, and her long hair, down to the small of her back, was disheveled and knotted. Tears of black makeup ran down her face. Her skin was not smooth as I expected, but laced with claw marks; some superficial wounds, others deep gouges. They littered her entire body and black liquid slowly oozed from the fresh wounds. Around the bottom of her neck, like a choker necklace, was a thick trench. Though her body peeled and bled, her face was tranquil as she handled the figurines with grace.

She pulled her attention away from the cabinet. "Oh!" Though she sounded surprised, her face remained solemn. "Jane is glad to see you again."

"Jane, what happened to you?"

She closed the cabinet door. "It was best for Jane to leave forever. It was just too much. When Father was around it was better, but when he was gone it was worse." Her white eyes glowed in the dark. She moved closer to me, but I moved back. "Jane couldn't see, but it was all too much for her. Father left her. He knew."

"Knew what?"

"That little Janey's skin was too tight and her head was on wrong," my sister whispered.

"What?" I asked again. There was a pause. Then Jane looked at the floor and started to respond in a voice too low for me to hear. I asked, "What did you see?" a bit more loudly as I stepped forward. As I got closer, I realized that she wasn't speaking, but singing in a child's voice.

"Little Janey, clothes don't fit right, skin's too tight, and her head's on wrong."

"What? Jane, I need to know what he knew and what you saw!" I said with a little more panic in my voice.

"Little Janey, clothes don't fit right, skin's too tight, and her head's on wrong. Little Janey, clothes don't fit right, skin's too tight, and her head's on wrong."

With harrowing persistence, she just kept repeating it over and over in her little sing-song voice, and increasingly became faster and louder. "Little Janey, clothes don't fit right, skin's too tight, and her head's on wrong.

LittleJaneyclothesdon'tfitrightskin'stootightandherhead 'sonwrong."

"Jane! What is wrong with you?!"

As I touched her to shake her, her head snapped up with a bone chilling pop, and she looked right at me while still singing that incessant tune. To my horror, she gave me the same, hollow-eyed stare as the figurines from the cabinet, with a vacant smile twisted on her face.

"LITTLEJANEYCLOTHESDON'TFITRIG HTSKINSTOOTIGHTANDHERHEADSONWRO NG!" now shouting through the smile. She bent her head down to one side in an unnatural way, mutilating her neck. The wounds on her skin began to leech even more dark blood, pooling underneath her feet and spoiling the rug, which hissed as the dark blood seeped through. I began to shake her violently, as if that would shake the madness from her. Her head bobbed back and forth like a rag doll as she continued her maniacal chant.

"LITTLEJANEYCLOTHESDON'TFITRIG HTSKINSTOOTIGHTANDHERHEADSONWRO

NG!" Jane convulsed under my palms, and I wasn't sure if I was shaking her or she was attacking me. She slapped my hands off her shoulders and knocked me back. When I looked up, there was a fiery glow in her eyes, and her smile was as wide as the gash in her neck. I wanted to jump up and help her, but the way she was leering at me with those orange eyes kept me glued to the spot. "HER SKIN'S TOO TIGHT! HER SKIN'S TOO TIGHT!" she screamed as she lunged at me. I threw my hands up to protect myself, but just then the cabinet light went out, and Jane went silent. A few seconds later, the hallway light flickered on. My sister was gone with nothing but out of place figurines as evidence that she was ever there.

The cold front began to wane, and the warmth of the house began to take its hold once again, but what I had seen in the cold left its mark on me. My legs were wobbly, barely usable, as I refused to look at the figurines in the cabinet on my way to the next room.

What frightened me more was in the living room. My mother was propped up in her armchair with a heavy blanket; nothing out of the ordinary. However, the television remote control was on her side table, where it was never placed. It was always in her hand or on an arm of her chair within reaching distance. But, between my mother and the television was Valery, sitting on a short ottoman that was usually attached to the sofa. I had interrupted a conversation between the two of them, for they suddenly fell quiet, and I had a strange feeling they were talking about me. Valery gave a gleeful smile, her cheeks dimpling. I inspected her, expecting her eyes to go wild again, but she merely sat innocently with her knees touching and her feet pointed inward. Even my mother seemed appeased, as much as she could ever be. The scene was impossible; my mother and my girlfriend together on their own accord. I narrowed my eyes at them, waiting for anything else out of the ordinary. "Valery," I said, "what are you doing here?" It was harsher than I had anticipated. My nerves had spilled into my voice.

She cocked her head. "What do you mean? I've been coming here more often than ever to help out since you've been able to take extra shifts. Why are you acting all weird?"

I ignored her question. "Is that right, Mom?"

My mother grunted in response, but said nothing else.

I didn't know what to say. One moment they were at each other's throats, and now they were acting overly cordial to one another. I feared Valery would lash out at me if I approached any closer, but she seemed calm and normal.

"We were just talking about how you are so much like your father," Valery said. "He sounds like an interesting man, if only I could have met him..."

I peered down at her, hoping to see a glint of something, so I knew what I was experiencing was purely my imagination. I didn't know what I wanted anymore; whether this was the truth or not. I saw nothing in her bright eyes, and I couldn't understand whether I should be relieved or even more terrified. Did she even remember that bloody night? She was acting like it never happened. Did it happen? Perhaps, just like my dream of St. Elizabeth's, that night was also a dream. So, if that didn't happen and the escapade in St. Elizabeth's and Dr. Lancaster didn't happen, then what was happening? What was the truth?

"Are you feeling alright, boy?" my mother asked. Her skin was putrid, more worn and tattered than normal. I was so surprised she asked about my well-being that I just stood there like a fish out of water floundering on the earth, out of my comfort zone.

Valery's face contorted in worry and she said, "Maybe I should get you something, you seem unwell." She gave a weak smile and went to the kitchen. I watched her go before I sat down in her place on the ottoman.

"Mom, what the hell is going on?" Fear pierced my skin, leaving goosebumps. My mother's nasty attitude had disappeared completely, and in its place was the psyche of a child as if terrified of a nightmare.

"Something is happening," she croaked. "I've felt this before. This cold terror that I can't shake." She rustled her blanket. "No matter how many layers I add." She grabbed my shoulders, pulling me closer to her. "The last time I felt this was when your father was still here. Just before everything went bad. It's happening again." She looked me over, her white eyes searching with urgency. "What happened to your hand?"

I pulled up my newly bandaged hand and said, "Just got some scratches."

Her eyes went wild. "Boy, did you do this? Was this you? Did you hurt yourself? That's where it starts, I've seen this before!"

"No!" I retaliated, annoyed she didn't believe me.

"Oh God." Her eyes began to tear. "Don't leave me," she said in despair. "I don't want you to leave me too. Always remember, no one will love you like I can."

"Except me," came Valery's voice. Her tone was on the brink of aggression, but her face remained as gorgeous and innocent as ever. "Here." Valery went to my side, holding out her fist and dumping four pills into my open palm. "Take these, and don't forget this." She gave me a glass of water, "Go on, it'll help."

"Don't take them!" my mother shrieked, gritting her teeth at Valery, "She's trying to take you away from me! I'm his mother," she spat at Valery. "I'm the one who's supposed to take care of my baby."

The sudden outburst from my mother did not faze Valery. The same stoic control Valery displayed did not likewise instill in me. Finally, the curtain had been drawn. She hated Valery because she was afraid Valery would become more important to me than her. The fear my mother possessed was abandonment. As time went on, Valery would pull me away from her. Anger simmered. "You? Take care of me?" I shouted. My mother glared back at me in a huff. "Who's been working a full time job and gambling at night to pay for your home while you sit back in your chair? I come here almost every day to check on you, cook for you, and feed you."

My mother was at a loss for words, and Valery remained silent, watching the events unfold with one raised eyebrow and a half smile as if egging me on. I don't know what spurred such ferocity in me. Maybe it was my splitting headache. I was constrained; tethered to my mother. It was a similar feeling that I had in my dream in St. Elizabeth's. The dread of being chained, controlled, and forgotten. Here, at least, I could walk right out the door.

"Do you know why Jane left? Do you, Mom?" My mother's eyes widened, exposing the whites of her eyes. "Your daughter left because of *you*. You pulled too tight, and she couldn't stand it anymore. *I* can't stand it anymore."

I fell silent, turning inward. My head felt like it was being split open with a blunt spoon. I wanted it to be gone, just like everything else shitty that's been happening. I just wanted it all gone. I fingered the pills in my hand, toying with the idea of it all ending.

In the window, I saw orange slits and a horrible mangled boney claw, dripping with rot, against the glass. Its sharp talon tickled the glass as it leered through those slits.

I popped the pills in my mouth, and downed them dry.

Chained

"See? Was that so hard?" I heard a woman's calming voice above me.

I felt my throat gurgle as the tablets scratched their way down into my system. My head was airy, and my eyes were unfocused. Every second my vision became clearer, and my eyes sensed brightness.

"We need to keep you on a strict timeline. Your medication will make you feel better, and will keep you here and lucid." Above me loomed a gorgeous young woman. Her face was kind and she had a smile that marked her cheeks with soft dimples that were further accentuated by piercings. "Valery?" I asked, recognizing her.

She seemed uncomfortable as her eyelashes sliced the air, looking about the room. She hushed me and said, "You should probably call me Nurse Malim out here." She leaned in closer, whispering into my ear. Her breath tickled with seduction. "What you did to me in the closet the other day.... Well, let's just say I'm looking forward to the next time." I was bewildered by her statement. I had no recollection of being with her in a closet. "I can hardly sit!" She winked at me and I felt my cheeks burn.

She returned her attention back to the trolley,

which had several trays with pills and tiny cups of water. They were all labeled specifically for each patient and I recognized names like William, Raymond, Daniel.... My mouth was parched, and the pills still felt like they were lodged in my throat, so I reached out for another cup of water.

But I couldn't. All this time, I was so preoccupied with the dread that I was back in my dream that I failed to observe that I was strapped down into a wheelchair. My arms were taped down on the arms of the chair, and my legs were similarly wrapped together, holding me in place. I whimpered slightly at this realization, and the suffocating feeling of being trapped began its scavenge for my sanity. I remembered I had slipped on the cowboy hat, but I didn't realize I had been injured so irreparably. I sighed with relief when I realized I could wiggle all of my extremities, though the panic of being restrained did not ease.

"Can you get me out of here?" I asked Valery, who was hovering over her trolley.

She turned to me, worry edged in her eyes. "I'm afraid I can't. At least, not yet. Dr. Lancaster is afraid you might hurt yourself again. And honestly, me too. Why do you keep hurting yourself?"

I had no answer, for it wasn't I who was committing the damage to myself. She continued, "Well whatever the reason, you keep disappearing from us when you do. We're all worried for you. Isabel, Dr. Lancaster, me, and especially your mother."

My mother was stuck to her chair in a row house. If she cared about me, then it was only to suit her own needs. If I wasn't there to take care of her, who would be? "She's coming for a visit, and she should be here soon." She gave a patient, who I recognized as Sara, her medicine. She then asked Sara to open her mouth, checking whether she swallowed her pills. She left me alone, sitting helplessly in the wheelchair. She went about the room and gave other patients their pills, but I had more questions, and I wasn't going to wait any longer.

"Valery!"

I saw her stiffen, but she ignored my call and continued giving out pills. I called out again, and once more she ignored me. I searched around the room. I saw Brian standing behind the front desk, ignoring what was happening in the room in front of him. Isabel was nowhere to be seen, and Dr. Lancaster was likely in his office. The only person that I could readily capture their attention was Valery, but she was ignoring me too.

Flustered, my blood began to pump faster and harder. I felt the blood flow to my veins in the wrist being stifled by the restraints. Blood pooled in my hand. It felt like lead, and my arm was burning and itching again. I knew, even if I itched it, the pain wouldn't be relieved. But still, I needed to scratch at it. My brain knew it wouldn't work, but my heart longed for relief.

The air increasingly seemed thinner, and with each breath I took I progressively lacked the necessary oxygen to survive. Each breath was simply not enough to fill my lungs sufficiently. Sweat pooled over my brow, and my heart was still pumping too hard. I pulled at my restraints, lightly at first, but then began to yank them as hard as I could. The thin fabric pinched my skin even more, but I pushed harder, gasping for air. I couldn't handle it any longer and I began to writhe and shake, hoping to twist and force my way out of the wheelchair. I shook so much that the wheelchair wobbled and toppled over. My shoulders braced my fall, though I felt the crunch, and my head only grazed the floor.

Some patients began to laugh, while others began to scream in hysterics. My mouth was planted on the cold marble floor, and I could do nothing but gasp for air. The moisture from my breath instantly wetted the floor, edging underneath my cheek. Against the will of every cell in my body, I held my breath. The last time I was hurt was a ticket back. I waited... waited to be sent away from there and back to reality, where the real Valery waited for me. Where my mother sat in her chair, barking and shouting at me. I didn't want to be here... unless here was real.

I was pulled away from my damp despair, and

my wheelchair set right. Seeing Valery's beautiful face tarnished with worry finally broke me. I wept into her arms as she wrapped herself around me. "I can't do this," I said into her armpit. "I can't be here! I'm not supposed to be here." She leaned back, so I could see her face, and I told her, "You're not supposed to be here," my voice cracking and giving out. "You don't work at St. Elizabeth's. Isabel and Brian are mentally ill patients, and Dr. Lancaster is a hobo on the street, not a doctor. And I've seen... it."

She embraced me again. "Oh honey, I wish it were true, but this is where we are. What have you been seeing? I've been here for almost as long as you've been here. I remember when I first saw you, I came up to you asking questions about St. Elizabeth's. It was only the next day when I was told you weren't another employee, but, in reality, a patient. You were so kind to me. I asked to see you on my breaks in 2B; your sector. They said you were happier and more stable when I was around; Dr. Lancaster found it prudent to transfer me here to 2B. As for Dr. Lancaster, he's been at St. Elizabeth's for over thirty years now. He's a fine man, a good man who I trust will do what is best for his patients, and that includes you." She touched my cheek, entirely ignoring the room filled with people "This is where you are meant to be. I'm with you now. Nothing can hurt you, not while you're here and not while I'm here. What you're running from won't find you here."

Duplicity

I was stuck. Fastened, glued, and restrained. My insolence in the public area had pinned me to my room, where at last I was freed from my wheelchair prison, but instead sentenced to solitude. Though the wheelchair waited for me, just outside my door. I saw it through the bars and knew it was laughing at me. I could tell it waited, yearned... desired for me to be one with it again. It frightened me. With its mouth agape, ready for me to be fastened in, it was difficult to ignore its presence just a few meters away.

My arm itched, and my nails dug into my skin. My entire forearm was bruised from the amount of scratching I had done, but I didn't care.

I heard voices, but not near the door. I looked up and saw a metal vent. I heard something like my name. It piqued my interest, so I pushed the desk to the wall. On top of the desk, I pressed my ear to the vent, listening to the conversation.

"How's he doing?" It was my mother's voice, but it wasn't her words. They were words she would never have uttered, and I immediately thought she was an imposter of some kind. But, as I listened on, her voice was every way my mother's.

"He's doing well," said Dr. Lancaster's voice.

"He is as healthy as you and me, but unfortunately, as we suspected, there has been no change in his behavior as his mind seems to be still locked. Treatments have not been able to reach him."

"I know," my mother seemed to whisper, though her voice carried well through the vent. "And what about my boy? How is he? Happy?"

Dr. Lancaster sighed, then took a deep breath. "I daresay he has illustrated to us that he is capable of delusions. We are trying to free him of this but it's not easy when he doesn't take his medication. Unfortunately, his medication can only be given orally, and if he is in the wrong mindset, he is able to either vomit it out or manipulate the nurses into thinking he swallowed. Cooperation is difficult. But, I assure you, the pills *do* work, and we have seen great changes in his behavior lately now that he's been recently more willing to take his medication. Nurse Malim is important to him, perhaps from a place of puerile misconception, but nevertheless I believe her presence will only facilitate his treatment."

I looked down at the place where the desk had been and saw a cracked square on the floor. Using my nails, I pulled on the square to reveal a bulging sock. When I opened it, I saw it was filled with half-digested pills. I didn't remember any of it. Someone else must have been hiding their pills... in my room; locked and restricted to every other patient.... Not willing to believe, I resumed my place on the desk, listening.

"It's been a few months now. Have you found out what's wrong with him?"

"Much like his family heritage, it seems he expresses signs of paranoid schizophrenia with extreme delusions." Dr. Lancaster seemed to have an answer for everything; clearly he was an idiot if he thought I was schizophrenic. What I saw was real.

My mother stammered in controlled fear. "What kind of delusions?"

"He claims he's one of the staff members of this establishment."

"Oh, that's not so bad," came my mother's sigh of relief.

"Maybe not, but he recognizes people here as if they were from a different life. Frankly, this is quite normal for him to use people around him as outlines for his delusions. It provides safety and control when his mind is at the helm. To him, we're the ones who aren't right. And of course, he frequently mentions a demon of sorts, a monster that is haunting his every step. Ma'am, it's alright, here take this. It's all in his mind, and I can assure you when he takes his pills, he is much more lucid. We will keep him on his regimen."

"The pills," my mother said in accusation, "you've said that before, that they'd work. They didn't, did they?"

"For most, they work beyond all belief. For some, it can control the symptoms, the delusions, but these people need more courage to prevail over their condition. It comes down to the individual."

"And what about my son? Can he prevail?"

There was a pause where Dr. Lancaster exhaled. "I don't know. We are here to support him but, ultimately, that... is up to him."

A Breath of Air

I touched the handle of the door to the hallway for the last time. My arm ached and itched, but I was able to open the door only once. I turned back around to gaze fondly over what had been my room over countless days and nights. Acceptance was the first step toward my recovery, but now I almost felt as if I was leaving something of myself behind; something I cherished dearly, but old and retired like a treasured yet long forgotten and overused toy of childhood.

I clutched the prescription bag Valery had left for me. She would meet me later tonight for dinner, once her shift was over. I stopped by the lobby, watching those who had yet to find themselves. I rang the bell for assistance, and Patty entered the caged desk area. "Hey!" he exclaimed, drawing fake pistols from his hips, "Pow pow! Gotcha! Guess you're not packing today, eh?"

Politeness forced a chuckle out of me. "No," I said. "Don't have much on me."

Patty smiled. "Yeah, but I bet you're aching to get out of here." He leaned in, closer to the bars that protected him from the crazies. "Just so we're clear. You've done a swell job. I'm proud of you. Beyond all odds, you powered through. Guess it's time to go out there and make something of yourself now, isn't it? Guess you're going to your mom's?"

"I guess," I said.

"Between you and me, maybe consider getting an apartment sometime. I think it could be good for you. I heard they're going to make the park into an apartment complex."

I nodded to him, then took a deep breath and exhaled as if I was preparing to run a marathon. The door buzzed and I left. I thought it would've been harder—or easier... I didn't know exactly what to expect.

Dawn was breaking, but the light fixtures on my way home still illuminated my way to my mother's. The air was warm now, and the dead leaves that had littered the streets had been replaced with tiny white flower petals. Fall and winter were worn and spring had its hold.

My mind briefly saw the horrific orange eyes that had once haunted me—but no longer. Not anymore. Not here. The thing couldn't find me here. What was before me was truly real, and monsters, ghosts, and ghouls were make believe. A contortion of reality filtered through my delusions. I knew that now, or at least I wanted to know that now.

I crinkled the bag containing my pills. The walk to my mother's was a little longer than I'd anticipated, and I had already passed my usual medication time. But it didn't matter. I would soon be at my mother's with a glass of water to ease the pills down my throat.

It had been quite a while since I had seen it last, but the row house was exactly as I remembered. I fumbled in my pockets and fished out my keys. Using the spare key, I opened the front door. I clenched my teeth; it still wasn't easy to only open it once.

No ghoulish figure of my sister waited for me. Only the television where I knew my mom was sleeping jabbered in the living room. But I felt out of place. I've been in this exact spot thousands of times, and yet I felt like I was in outer space; adrift and untethered. The portraits of family and friends were hammered into the walls in their normal places, but the frames were different and alien. Everything was in its place, but the details were not quite as I remembered. The long, worn hallway rug was in need of a vacuum, but it was as I mostly remembered. It felt like my old home, but how my memory had lapsed over the weeks and months of being away.... I looked down at the keys I still hadn't placed back into my pocket. There was the bronze key I used to enter my mother's house, a few grocery store benefit cards, and two other keys. One of them caught my eye. It was an old-fashioned barrel key; heavy and black. I knew what the key was for.

I looked down the hallway; empty and deserted. The display cabinet that my father had once placed his valuable figurines in was gone. The wall where it was bolted to was clean and untarnished, as if it had never been there in the first place, a notion that was realistically impossible. Immediate anger boiled in me. How could my mother trash something my father and, to a certain extent, I myself had treasured?

I stormed into the living room where my mother was sleeping in her chair. "How could you get rid of that cabinet?"

She woke up with a start, and I was surprised to see her agility had returned since I had last seen her. She seemed younger and fitter. She smiled, ignoring the status of my mood, and reached out for a hug. "I'm so glad to see you! I'm so proud of you; you did it!"

While I reciprocated the hug, I did not cool my anger. "Where are the figurines? The cabinet?"

She stepped back with apprehension. "Your pills, are those your pills?" she asked, pointing to the bag in my hand, "Maybe you should take one. Are you sure they let you out? I didn't get a phone call..."

"Mom, the cabinet. Where the fuck is the cabinet?"

"Oh, honey. What cabinet?" There was only truth in her eyes, heavily tarnished with disappointment.

"The cabinet, with all of Dad's figurines." I pulled out my keys and held the one that unlocked the cabinet. "See?" I said, stuffing it under her nose. "See!?"

My mother shook her head in remorse. "There was no cabinet. That key doesn't belong here. Maybe I should call Dr. Lancaster..." She turned to the phone on the side table by her chair. Quickly, before she was able to dial the number, I swiped the phone and threw it across the room, where it smashed into pieces against the wall. Her eyes flashed orange with warning. My mind skipped and clicked.

"Jane," I said. "Tell me about Jane."

She lifted a hand and the fire across my cheek burned. "How dare you bring her up."

I had half a mind to swipe back at her. Instead, I leered at her with my fist white as bone, demanding she tell me what had happened to her. She bit her cheeks, and her shoulders slumped. "She was the happiest of people. She lit up the room like nothing else would. She had a way with your father that no one, not even me, had. Your father had his troubles, but whenever she was around, it was as if those delusions didn't exist. She meant so much to him... and me. But I've learned that especially the happiest of us might be suffering underneath more than those who suffer outwardly."

"Tell me," I whispered. "I need to know what happened. For once, just tell me."

Her apprehension rose, but she continued against her judgment. "Your sister, especially when your father disappeared from us days at a time, locking himself away... she deteriorated... mentally unstable. It went unnoticed at first. She smiled just as often with such exuberance, but behind the curtain, she was falling apart. When your father was present, and in his right mind, it seemed to give her the focus she needed to push through. Still, something was dragging her down, and though she tried, it ended up being too much for her. Though she smiled, such a beautiful joyous smile, inside I knew she was dying. At the end, a knife to her own throat was what relieved her pain and affirmed mine."

The Itch

I locked myself in the bathroom to take a breather and think. Sitting on the toilet, I inspected the keys dangling in my hand. Perhaps it was because I hadn't taken my medication recently... or perhaps my mother was lying. There *was* a cabinet. How else would I have the key? The key existed, which meant there was a cabinet, but the cabinet wasn't here. And it dawned on me... if the cabinet wasn't here... then it was *there*. The place I had overcome. The place I had escaped. The place that wasn't real, where the monster lay in wait to haunt me.

I looked in the rusted and grimy mirror; hopeless to fix. My face looked gaunt and my nose was more hooked than I remembered. It reminded me of Isabel and her strange warning. Listen and learn, or ignore and endure. "FACE IT" reverberated in my skull. It banged against my brain loud enough to crack my skull and all the while my arm itched and ached. I had been on my pill regimen when the wheelchair man had made his warning. It was all gibberish then, but now it seemed clearer as if a fog had been lifted or a semi-opaque curtain had been cast aside to sharpen my resolve.

The wheelchair man, Isabel, Brian, and the

hobo on the street all knew. They had seen what I saw. They had the ability to see, it was a gift, while the others like Dr. Lancaster, Valery, and my mother, were so shut down and removed from reality that their tunnel vision could not allow them to see what we saw. They were ordinary. The facts that were right in front of them; they simply could not comprehend and were blind to see what lay beneath the shadows.

There was a rap at the door and my mother's voice said, "Honey, I just got off the phone with Dr. Lancaster. There was an incident... honey, just open the door, can we just talk?" I refused her request, and said instead, "Who? What kind of incident?"

"Nurse Malim.... I'm so sorry, Honey, but Dr. Lancaster said it was serious. Do we have to do this through the bathroom door?" She sighed. "Something happened to Nurse Malim, baby. She tried to slit her throat, is in critical condition in the hospital."

"What?" I snapped. "What do you mean, gone?" I had fought against my nature and escaped the horrible hospital, only to find myself wishing I were back where I used to be; whether it be reality or a figment of my delusions, I didn't care, as long as I was back with her.

"...I'm so sorry, Honey..." My mother kept talking, but I didn't hear anything more. I was numb. Maybe because I had gotten better, the creature had found her instead... or it was always after her and I, taking my pills and not going back, allowed it to get to her? The light posts breaking in succession towards my apartment; the creature, watching from outside my apartment where Valery was waiting for me inside. It was after her and had always been after her. Not me.

I stared at myself in the mirror as I scratched my arm and threw my head forward into the glass. Shards sprayed the bathroom along with drips of my blood. I closed my eyes and hoped... but nothing happened. I clenched my fist and struck my own jaw. My brain sloshed within my skull. I recovered, but I was nowhere different. Every time I reverted back to the other place with the monster, I had injured myself, but it wasn't working this time; maybe it wasn't enough.

Were the pills impacting me? I had only been off them for a few hours now, would their potence degrade that quickly within my body?

Scratching my arm, another knock on the door shook me from my mind. "I saw you left your pills downstairs. Open the door so I can give them to you."

"It's fine, Mom! I have one," I said through the door.

"No you don't. The packs are all full."

"I took one of the packs," I said.

I swore under my breath, itching my arm. I looked down, inspecting it. All of this time it had consistently itched and burned. It was red, ugly, and bruised from my claws. As time went on, away from my pills, I was able to steadily increase clarity. While my mother was abated for the moment, she would be back to tempt me once again with the pills that clouded and impeded my clarity and led to naive obscurity.

"I wasn't there and I lost her here, there, and everywhere." The words of the wheelchair man guided my thoughts as if they were a compass that led me to my destination. I had no intention of becoming the man in the wheelchair. He knew he had to be somewhere else to fix everything, which meant I had to, too. The difference between him and I was that he failed.

I pulled open the medicine cabinet beside the broken mirror. Sharp scissors watched me as I gingerly reached for them. They were cold in my hand, and the burning of my arm needed their cold. I touched the blade against my skin, allowing blood to seep possessively over my bicep.

The scissors would not be enough. At that moment, my mother banged on the bathroom door. "Open this door! At least take your medicine! Just one pill. Honey? You're scaring me, please open the door. Open this door, or *I WILL!*"

I made no effort to respond to her wishes. And with a ferocious shout, a deep thick knife blade gouged its way through the door, splintering the wood. Like a woodpecker, my mother sliced and stabbed at the door. "I have to take care of you! No one can love you like I do! Not even her." I made no attempt to dissuade her as I stared at her through the splintering holes she was creating. When the door was practically in ribbons, I saw my moment and dove through the wood and tumbled into her. Exhausted from her barrage against the door, I easily disarmed her and retreated back to the bathroom, knife in hand.

I knew I was right. Isabel, the man on the tires, the wheelchair... everyone at the hospital... they were all right. I was not willing to risk Valery's life against it, but I was willing to risk mine for it.

I raised the knife high and plunged the blade deep into my arm. The blade hadn't extinguished the tenacious itch, so I pulled the blade back out from my flesh and raised it again while I watched my blood spill. My mother screamed out in agony and horror as I relentlessly chopped at my arm, which with each hack was beginning to feel better. Only pain was left behind as I had finally relieved the itch that had plagued me for so long. The knife clattered to the ground, next to my disembodied forearm. The waterfall of blood that had escaped me left me tired and worn, but it was enough to elicit a sense of euphoria while my eyelids forced themselves shut.

Together Again

Eyes opened, then clenched shut. It was too bright. It was so bright I could see the pink behind my eyelids. As my consciousness resumed in a snap, I sat upright and held out my arm. It was limp. I knew something was wrong, so very wrong. I clenched my upper arm, which I felt, but the rest of my arm down to my hand was completely numb. Forcing my eyes open again, I became jarred by the extra space where my arm and hand should have been. It made me dizzy and my eyes couldn't focus, as they expected something more to be there.

Focusing elsewhere, and on the task at hand, a glance at the time on my other wrist told me it was in the middle of Valery's night shift at the club. I tried not to look at my stump; the price to be where I was.

I made my way down the street where the street lights hummed. The cracks in the pavement looked as though they had been brutally repaired since I had been away. The pavement sealer seemed to have no effect, arguably stretching the cracks even wider than before. Potholes were ostensibly sealed, but when I stepped upon them, my foot crumpled inside them and it tore at my ankles. There was no repairing the road; nothing anyone could do now but allow nature's claws to devour it.

Patty greeted me as he always did outside the club. "Back so soon? Is everything okay?"

"No," I said, holding my anxiety at bay. "Valery... is Valery here?"

Patty's face relaxed in sympathy. "No she's not. She's been spotty at work, and when she's here, it's as if she's a ghost. She's paler than normal and heavy, as if something's been pulling her down. Have you been home lately?"

I shook my head. "No, I've been at my mom's."

He nodded. "Okay, 'cause I thought she was hanging around your place. I'd check there."

I didn't tell Patty that I had been evicted from my apartment. Instead, I thanked him and turned around, but he called out after me, so I turned back around. "It's dark out there. Too bad you aren't packing tonight."

With urgency, I retraced my steps, back the way I came, until my foot crunched; a ring of white glass. I slowly directed my eyes upward and saw that the street light had once again been blown out. I went on ahead, but saw that the next street light had suffered the same fate. The entire street, usually illuminated by the dim streetlights, was now encased in darkness.

And I knew, without a doubt, that it had been here. Those horrible orange eyes had been here.

Destroyed all of the light in front of it in a path that headed straight to my apartment; straight to Val. The monster had never been after me,-; I was just an obstacle in the way to its real prey. I ran full speed down the familiar street where I had first encountered the thing that stalked the one I loved most. "My baby girl, it took her from me," my father's voice echoed in my ears. I couldn't let it take Val, like it took my sister. My footsteps clashed against glass every few paces as I passed underneath each disintegrated street light.

Ahead of me, in the night that had won over the street lights, were black, billowing garments. There was a faint smell of perfume in the air. I crept forward, hoping she had not heard me approach. She was heading to the emergency stairwell toward my apartment.

"WRONG WAY!" The voice startled me. It was the hobo Dr. Lancaster atop his tower of tires. "Come back. You cannot be out here!" He pointed back from where I came. "I'm trying to help you! Go that way!"

"No!" I cried out, brandishing my fist with ire. "You can't make me!"

I saw the feminine figure halt, her garments billowing behind her as she turned for me. Her heels beckoned my attention as she approached.

"It's out of your hands," he said. "There's nothing you can do for her now. Just come back." But then my eyes lied to me and saw the clean shaven, carefully groomed Dr. Lancaster before me. "Listen, it's not real, it's not there! Focus!" But I couldn't. The beautiful woman held my attention. The hook in her nose was cast by a shadow and disappeared as she threw down her garments, revealing Nurse Malim underneath. Her face was contorted with worry and she went to stand by Dr. Lancaster, who had stepped down from his tower of tires. They both turned and began to approach me slowly, almost threateningly.

"I know you see things," she said to me. "You are special, you can see things most cannot, but that doesn't mean they are real."

"They *are* real!" I said, pointing to the glass on the ground that the orange-eyed thing had surely left behind. "You see that?" I asked and they looked down. "Do you see that!? That was the Creature!!"

With direct repose, Dr. Lancaster said, "There is always something else that explains these abnormalities that you perceive. In this case, the street lights have had recent maintenance by an inexperienced electrician, who happens to have worked at St. Elizabeth's. I was notified of similar electrical issues at the hospital, and an investigation found it was this exact inexperienced individual. You see? What you think is some demonic creature is in fact a malfunction born from a living human being and nothing more. You didn't know this because I never thought it prudent to tell patients of inconsequential irritations. If I had known it vexed you enough to spur your delusions, I would have explained this much earlier..."

Nurse Malim joined in, her eyes flashing orange. "What Dr. Lancaster is trying to tell you is that what you are experiencing, the things you might think you are seeing, is only your mind making up a story where an explanation can't be found. There is always an explanation."

"You're wrong!" I spat. "And you're not Nurse Malim. The real Valery needs me!" Nurse Malim snarled, her upper lips quivering. Her orange eyes intensified.

I tore myself away from them toward my apartment, but I heard in the distance, "Wrong way! Go *that* way!" And the tapping of heels sharply increased, then with a whoosh of wind went silent.

I raced ahead, not willing to linger any longer. I climbed the emergency stairwell and pressed my face against the glass window of my apartment. I saw Valery, sitting hunched on the sofa with her head between her knees. I tapped on the glass to notify her of my presence without startling her. Her neck craned up and I saw the beautiful dimpled smile I missed so desperately, but her eyes were shallow and the circles under them frightened me. She stood and limped toward the glass, cradling her wrist as her blood trickled down her arm to her elbow, soaking her rolled up sleeve. She took her finger and dipped it in, and to my horror, began to write on the glass.

"I can't…" she spelled. "Hold on."

I shouted out to her, but she seemed to not hear me. Instead, I banged on the glass with my fist as hard as I could, but the glass would not break. It wouldn't even splinter into webs like the mirror in my apartment. "STOP!" I screamed as loud as I could through the glass. She dipped her finger in the blood again and drew a bleeding heart. She placed her palm on the glass and I pressed mine against hers. Only a thin piece of glass between us. Looming above her, orange eyes lit like fire in the dark room. Rotten flesh from its face dribbled onto her shoulders. In a flash of darkness, it raked her back, then sent her body forward onto the glass. I saw her eyes become vacant with immense pain. With a blast, the creature tore her. Blood sprayed the glass, obstructing my view. A gnawed arm bone, with chunks of flesh still attached, soared through the glass, finally breaking it.

Her body landed in a shredded, bloody heap. Her face was untarnished, beautifully staring. My footing was lost as I slipped in Valery's blood and fell on her mutilated body, my face, inches away from hers. Her lips still trembled and pulsated and her eyes twitched.

My back seared in pain. I pushed myself away from Valery's corpse, but didn't have time to roll over. Instead, I looked up and behind me. And, above, leered the monster with its hooked beak opened into a glacial smile. One of its talons was covered in my blood. It raised the talon in preparation for a strike. Fear forced my body to stand and I darted for the bathroom. The claw-like talon plunged into Valery's corpse instead of me. I heard the gush of flesh. In wretched anger, it pulled out Valery's lungs, forcibly spraying blood. It cackled, and with a sickening squish, it clenched its talon and crushed Valery's lungs into pieces. I pushed forward to the bathroom, but the thing clawed at my shoulders, weighing me down and raking me backwards. I lost my footing again and toppled over Valery's corpse again, this time with a massive cavity in her chest. She was beautiful; unmoving and hideous. My arm and elbow pushed down into her to pull myself up, her vertebrae scraping my skin. The creature, distracted by Valery's body, released me and pulled on her leg instead. And with a sickening crunch, it broke her leg and began to bite and slither its tongue around her flesh.

Frantically, I raced to the bathroom door, where the mirror that could never be cleaned would be my haven from the beast. I lurched forward, feeling the monster breathing on me. As I locked the door behind me, the door bulged inward from the force of the monster. The door's hinges almost broke, but the thing did not knock it down. Instead, it began to toy with me. Tease me into a sense of dread and despair that it knew would drive me crazy. Each toying scratch and tapping it made on the door pricked my brain. Both of us knew I was caught. There was no escape. Except... maybe one.

I dug my hand into my pocket and withdrew a loose pill and clenched it between my fingertips. My spine constricted as the thing outside scraped its talon from the top of the door slowly down to the bottom. I raised my trembling stump. My vision was blurred by splinters and I felt its talons clasp my ankles. Tightly they squeezed, hooks digging through my bone, and then with a quick thrust, cracked them like twigs. An alarm, and I knew my time had ended.

Vacant Infinity

I looked out from familiar large windows behind a latticework of steel in a quiet and clean hallway. Rain droplets on the window fell into one another in a cascading torrent, desperately holding on to the glass so as to not plummet to the ground. When it all became too heavy, it would drop and disappear below the line; forgotten and never seen again.

Next to me was a familiar figure, equally restrained in a wheelchair, equally sullied and worn. And together, we looked out from inside the glass, like figures resting in a glass cabinet.

END